City of Stories

City of Stories

First published in Great Britain in 2017 by Spread the Word

Design by Franek Wardynski
franekwardynski.com

ISBN13: 978-1-9998254-0-9

Supported using public funding by
**ARTS COUNCIL
ENGLAND**
LOTTERY FUNDED

Contents

Foreword

This fantastic collection of diverse and punchy stories have been created as part of City of Stories, a London-wide creative writing project celebrating London's libraries, writers and readers. City of Stories is managed by London's writer development agency Spread the Word, in partnership with the Association of London's Chief Librarians. Spread the Word help London's writers make their mark on the page, the screen and in the world. City of Stories is funded by Arts Council England Grants for the Arts.

Throughout June 2017, twenty library services across London flung open their doors to writers, aspiring writers and those-who-never-thought-of-themselves-as-writers for free creative writing workshops. At forty free writing workshops, 450 adults took part in stimulating, fun and exploratory writing exercises facilitated by the fantastic pool of City of Stories writers 2017; City of Stories writers in residence Bidisha, Alex Wheatle, Irenosen Okojie and Courttia Newland, and City of Stories writers Tom Mallender, Lewis Buxton, Laila Sumpton, Jasmine Cooray, Miriam Nash, Anita Belli and Nick Field, ably supported by Erica Masserano.

Workshop participants were invited to enter the City of Stories competition which asked for 500 word stories. 500 word stories sound easy to write? They're really not! Over 200 people entered the competition anonymously, and judges Bidisha, Courttia Newland and Irenosen Okojie were overwhelmed with the talent and creativity of entries. Somehow, they honed the entries down to winners and highly commended writers for each Borough of London that took part in City of Stories. The winners for each Borough and between one and three highly commended stories, form the main content of this book. We're also delighted to feature new stories by the four City of Stories writers-in-residence alongside the 60+ winning City of Stories 500 word stories.

This anthology takes you on a journey across London—starting in the North, moving through East then South and finishing in West London. Amongst the many themes and topics explored by the anthologised stories, you'll be welcomed into worlds featuring dragons, animals, anxiety, family recipes, immigration and much more. We should warn you that some of the stories feature strong language.

City of Stories will return to libraries across London in 2018, as will the second edition of this anthology. If you are reading this after then, know that this two-year project has celebrated London's writers, readers and libraries.

Congratulations and thank you to all the winning and highly commended writers anthologised in this book, and to you, the reader, enjoy travelling on a literary journey across London created by over 60 talented writers. You can read more about the writers at the back of this book, and check out the acknowledgements page where we tip our caps to the vast number of people who made City of Stories and this book happen. I'll end with the great words of Bidisha:

'The stories cover numerous times and a panoply of places, but each have something in common: the writer is a great new voice.'

Laura Kenwright
Spread the Word
September 2017
#cityofstories / spreadtheword.org.uk

When the Bombs Stop Falling

—BIDISHA

Inspired by the wartime testimonies of Ben Sacks, James Elgar, Doris Cosgreave and Inge Munroe, which can be heard at the museum in The Library at Willesden Green, and by letters preserved in the Brent archives on the same site.

Irene made a wish as her brother Jem carved the turkey: the war would end and Father would come home. The following Christmas there was no turkey and Jem himself had gone to fight.

Irene spent New Year's Eve outside, watching the searchlights pick out enemy bombers. A lorry turned into the street, pulling an anti-aircraft gun behind it. The soldier manning the gun let a long peal of rounds into the sky and the lorry sped on. Irene saw bombers gathering overhead.

'Get inside!' shouted her mother. 'They think there's a gun emplacement here!'

They had a few seconds before the bombs hit.

That spring, Jem came home for three days.

'I'm going to design a tank that ends the war,' said Irene. 'It'll jump trenches, go underground and swim through water.'

'Tanks are useless,' Jem laughed. 'Most of them break down the minute they're on the field and the others collapse under fire.'

A tank testing centre opened up the road in Dollis Hill. Irene wanted see if her tank could be made for real, so she waited for her mother to go to sleep, took a butter knife for self-defence and climbed the hill. The centre was surrounded by watchtowers and wire.

'What are you doing?' hissed the night guard.

Irene started trembling.

'I wanted to see if there's a tank that'll win the war and… and bring my father back. He's a pilot. I made a wish at Christmas—the Christmas before last.'

Luckily, the guard was kind.

'We've just the thing. Come with me.'

In the warehouse sat a massive metal tank.

'That,' announced the guard, 'is the Mark 9. One look at that and the enemy will surrender. What's more, it was made in your own back yard.'

Jem died in the war and Irene heard nothing more about the Mark 9. Father sent letters home, written in pencil in a sloping hand on porous pages torn from a notebook.

Irene's mother sold her jewellery and house ornaments. Irene looked after the rationing book, keeping track of the points they'd used on tinned food and the weekly coupons for sugar, butter and bread. She dreamed about breakfasting on fresh eggs and sausages—no chance when the meat ration was one shilling per person per week.

Irene's mother began work in the munitions factory, making shell cases for torpedoes. It was heavy work for two pounds a week. She and the other women built air raid shelters in the garden and laid sandbags over the top.

Every day the factory gave its workers a half hour break. A local lady, Aunt Rose, collected ration coupons from each woman, bought cheap cuts of oxtail and liver and made tasty stews for everyone.

'When you join together, things go further. It's the single people that struggle on one ration,' said Rose one lunchtime when Irene was helping her serve.

Suddenly, they heard doodlebugs overhead.

'Don't worry,' said Rose. 'As long as you can hear the engine running, you're safe because you know it's going to go past you.'

The engines cut out. They ran to the shelter, the doodlebugs went into a nosedive and the neighbours at 74 and 76 Church Road got a direct hit. Then came the V2 rockets, which struck with no warning. The houses crumbled on top of the shelter and trapped everyone inside for two days.

Irene was evacuated to the seaside. She was allowed a change of clothes, her nightie and underwear, handkerchiefs and a family photograph. She lived for letters from her parents. Her father addressed her as Fluff, her childhood nickname, and wrote, 'You are clearly getting some benefit from the sea air, and yes I think you are putting on flesh if you are over eight stone.'

Irene ran away, came home to London and visited the war office.

'I'll do anything,' she told the man at the desk.

'Civil defence need messengers. Can you ride a bicycle?'

'I'll learn.'

'Then get yourself to Tailors Lane. Place called The Hub.'

The Hub was an ordinary office at street level but underground were dozens of operators wearing headphones, sitting at desks plugged with wires.

'It's a telephone exchange,' explained the woman showing Irene around. 'We take incident calls and send help: heavy rescue, light rescue and ambulances. If the lines are down, we use messengers. That's you.'

Irene crossed the city, pedalling wherever she was sent to deliver messages. Gradually she made friends with the 'ATS girls'—young women from the Auxiliary Territorial Services.

'We need someone for the quartermaster department. Like wardrobe. You'd be giving us our shoes and socks,' said a Lancashire girl called Sally.

On her first day, Irene found everyone lined up outside the nurse's office.

'Head inspection,' said Sally. 'They're saying we've got lice. Especially us from industrial parts. Nurse is a snob, she thinks we sleep in hovels, five to a bed.'

The common room stank of chemicals and the girls sat about glumly, wearing towel turbans soaked in head lice treatment.

'We'll be like this for three days,' said Sally. 'It'll all go grand, 'til we go home on leave and come back just as lousy as before.'

In the last and bloodiest year of the war, Irene became an ambulance driver. She attended a midnight hit on Neasden sheds, where the carriages of the Metropolitan Line trains were kept. Then another call came through:

'String of bombs at Stone Bridge. The turning's demolished from one end to the next. Nothing's left.'

When Irene was twenty her childhood wish finally came true: the war ended and her father came back. Irene's mother opened a shop and her father became the local mayor. They died of old age.

Irene inherited her mother's business. She never married and lived in the same flat all her life. After she died, there was a house clearance. In a shoe box, next to her dentures and plastic rollers, was a bundle of letters addressed to Fluff.

Water
—ELIZABETH UTER

Water cascades down the building's face, spilling onto the pavement below. Stops to see if anyone observes. Then pours back
up the side to the roof, to begin the journey once more. Sliding in
a joyful 'whoosh' and repeating its upward course like an unruly
child, delighting in forbidden play. On the fourth or fifth turn, the
waterfall is aware of prying eyes. Stills to become ice, hanging
from the tiles.

Jens, from the house next-door, blinks his eyes, rubs them and
blinks again. He shakes his head but like a man drugged, desires
more. He leaves his window spy-hole and from a small attic
door creeps onto the roof. From his new post, he spies on the
ice block. The solidified form changes anew. The frozen outline
becomes a curvaceous woman shape. Jens crawls a little closer.
Only the boundary between the two roofs separate them.

Enraptured by this unearthly presence, this maiden carved in
ice. Jens waits awhile. At first, the time unmarked, then, glancing
at his watch, thirty, forty, fifty minutes idle by. Then an hour; two,
three and still the statue stands. Eerie, empty, still. Emboldened
now, Jens straightens from the confines of his hidey-hole. He
stretches his cramping legs. Gauges the distance between the
two buildings with both hands. Takes a few careful steps backwards then launches forward and jumps.

Jumping the gap seems like stretching the gap. Wider and
wider as his single leap becomes longer and longer. He sees
infinitely small details of the city amplifying before him. The big
bell in the church's tower has ten tones of bronze when before
his eye saw only one. Each and every blade of grass and grain of

earth, red, brown, black, grey, a limitless, teasing, variety of hues in Mr. Joe's immaculate, square lawn. Jens sees all the eggs in Aunt Marie's freshly baked cake as it cools at the kitchen window.

Turning his head, he nods. He knows a very distant neighbour is hanging a red 'kerchief on the line and that each thread, is like blood flowing through a thousand human bodies. He understands, as he lands on the other side, that he is glimpsing eternity. Walking without will towards the ice statue, he smells fragrant roses in a faroff field and it is as close to him now as it will ever be. As close as his own soul. He bends towards the Ice Queen, shrinking to his knees. His eyes focusing on her mouth.

Her lips come together. A smile that drags the warmth from him. Her breath gushes towards him, sweeping him away to the edge of the roof. He topples over. Not dying but flowing. Not touching earth, hurtling up. She reaches a hand to him. He takes it. They merge. Emptiness. There is nothing to remember but water. Being water. Falling water. Running water. Lastly, water—vapour—joining with the sky's essence, forever.

The Man Who Wanted to be a Tree

—KRISTEL TRACEY

He dug his toes into the copper-coloured earth, wriggling his feet until they sank into the wet soil. While the tropical rain drenched his upturned face, it broke into a broad smile as his arms reached up to the heavens. 'Home. I am home,' he said to the sky.

Shoes. They were the thing he hated most when he landed on the cold pavements of Britain as a 7-year-old, new leather brogues pinching his feet. Shoes symbolised hard church pews and school desks. Freedom was chasing his pet chicken around his aunt's farm and climbing pimento trees, bare feet impervious to sharp edges. 'Yuh cyaah run roun London barefoot like yuh back a bush, bwoy,'his mother chided.

Go home. He couldn't recall the number of times he'd been told that in his lifetime. Shouted at him in playgrounds, scratched into desks or Sharpied onto public toilet walls. 'I am home' he wrote back, a question mark hanging over his head like mistletoe to a kiss.

Years. As they passed, the longing for his birthplace subsided into a dull, unidentifiable ache. He ate his English breakfasts with a side of fried plantain. He still rooted for the West Indies in cricket or damn-near spontaneously combusted when Usain was racing. But he had papered over his accent long ago. He'd never gotten used to the momentary flash of shock that met him on customers' doorsteps, as they realised the face that greeted them didn't quite match the voice they'd spoken to over the phone.

Roots. He had laid roots in this land of opportunity. He had married and divorced here, borne children here, and witnessed the country develop into a place where his children rarely had their right to reside questioned. 'You still have to work twice as hard to get half as far as them,' he told his disbelieving offspring. 'Whatever, Dad.'

But as he got older, the winds pulling him from the West got stronger. He became weathered and weary until, one day, he decided to climb aboard the gusts.

As he clambered through the landscape of his childhood, he peered in wonder at the sights, smells, sounds and tastes that clung onto the edge of his memory. Names escaped him—'Is this guinep?' he asked himself, as he took a bite of the strange but familiar fruit.

As the raindrops descended on him and he sank deeper into the earth, he saw the question mark above his head wash away. 'Home. I am home.'

From afar, a pair of locals observed the man taking root in the middle of a yam field.

-'A weh dis yah half eediat cum fram?'

-'Him cum fram farin.'

*Fram farin = from foreign = from abroad!

Night Tube

—SINEAD BEVERLAND

Every Friday night for five weeks, he'd been watching her. She'd been alone up until now but tonight as he boarded the train, she was with a man. Her eyes were closed and she appeared to be sleeping, her head resting on the shoulder of this blonde interloper.

He tried not to stare but disappointment coursed through him as he took his usual seat opposite. From this position he could watch discreetly and curse himself for not acting sooner. He had planned on speaking to her tonight. He felt a fool. The whisky he'd drunk for courage coated his tongue, dragging it up and cementing it to the roof of his dry mouth.

People staggered on and off the carriage in various states of inebriation and the stench of lager clung to them like glue. She was different. She was composed and quiet. He always assumed she was on her way home from work and he'd decided that would be his first question. Not now though.

Where previously he had prayed for delays, he now craved someone would hit fast forward. The train jolted through the darkness and he self-consciously rose to his feet, making his way to the furthest door. His stop was next.

Stepping out on to the empty platform, he was home. The train sat, hovering, perhaps just for his benefit. He walked past their carriage. He wasn't strong enough not to look. It was his last opportunity. He paused at the window that framed them squarely together. They looked even more intimate from a distance, their eyes gently closed. He felt he was intruding and reluctantly walked away, consigning her to memory.

As the train left the station, she opened her eyes lazily and lifted her head. Looking up at the stranger next to her, she pressed her lips together and her cheeks flushed hotly. *Sorry*, she said, glancing at his shoulder. He smiled and shrugged, his eyes narrow with drink. She straightened in her seat, awkwardly embarrassed. Scanning the carriage she realised she'd missed her stop but more importantly she had missed him.

Earbuds
—CHARLOTTE FORFIEH

I've never liked trains, but this one is different. It carries me away from a small seaside town, away from Mum, her whispers and her tears.

Away from you.

Opposite me a young woman sprawls across two seats, cursing her phone's lost signal. Behind me an old couple chatter. I need my earbuds.

My hand reaches into my bag, pushes past a crumpled black suit, and hits something unfamiliar. I dig it out, a book with frayed binding: your diary. It looks work-a-day, cheap, like you.

I lean back in my seat as the memory of your last visit hits.

You'd scowled at the bill. 'How much?'

'Don't—' I'd said.

'Now listen here, Davy. That was a lovely breakfast but...'

'Brunch!' I shouted like a kid. I'd looked down at the organic left overs on my plate. 'It's fine.'

'Fine?' You scoffed. 'I don't think so. London... Why'd you ever move here?' You shook your head, said: 'I'll sort it,' and barked our server over.

'No,' I'd placed my wallet on top of the bill. '*It is fine.* And anyway, I can afford it.' A knock-out punch.

You shrugged and left the next morning—back to the sea. A gig had come up, but had it really? That's what you always said when you wanted out of things. A hurried goodbye, a door more slammed than shut. Adiós, Dad.

After the service, your friends offered their condolences. *What a top bloke he was*, they said, *and how talented*. Yeah right.

Your life was hemmed in by the sea. You chose fish and chips over fresh fettuccine; back-street bands over world-class art. Not for you a career, just a job for beer money. You hadn't travelled. Or studied. You'd never worn a suit until this morning.

I push your diary away and turn to the window. Power cables dissect the sky. They keep pace with the train as it rushes me back to my city.

In London, I leave the train and become one among millions. Anonymous.

I slip into the stream of people flowing towards Euston Square station, London's heavy air so welcome in my lungs.

A busker, half-sheltered from the rain, stands in a doorway, her guitar case open and hungry. I let your diary fall from my fingers and keep walking. It thuds into the case. No one says anything. No one sees. The music doesn't stop.

The first peal of thunder booms as I descend beneath the city. Your diary should be wet now, its secrets drowned or drowning.

Mum strove to bridge the empty space between you and me. She was always planting things, watering the soil between us. But our differences defined us, Dad. They held us in place.

On the platform I found my earbuds and plugged in.

Ab Alto (From Above)

—KIM HORROCKS

The small child is perching on a rickety and worn art deco dining chair in the front bedroom. She is looking into a mirror on the wall. She can barely see her reflection. The glass is opaque, scratched and seen much much better days. The blurred image beckons to her. She leans forward. She places her small hands flat on her cheeks, spreads out her fingers and pulls at the corners of her mouth.

There. A smile. Anything is possible.

In an unremarkable modern council house an old lady sits at her 1950's kitchenette eating cream crackers smothered in butter and dairy lea soft cheese. She looks at the clock above the cooker. Almost 7 o'clock.

She wipes the crumbs from her apron and mumbles to herself: 'Jack, you're late. Dear Jack, Where are you?' She tidies up the kitchenette and goes to sit down in front of the telly in the living room. She's watching 'Opportunity Knocks' and tut-tutting at the presenters pronunciations. Gal axe hey of stars squeals, Hughie Green, from one side of his mouth. A little dog sits on the floor next to her. Attuned.

The old lady looks at the clock above the telly. Almost 8 o'clock. She rubs her rheumatoid hands together. Her hands are so twisted. She loves oranges but has long ago given up trying to peel them. Sometimes she manages to cut them; once, twice… as many times as her fingers allow her. Jack likes to buy oranges on his way home from his day shift at the pit. 'Jack. You're so late.' She thinks. Worried.

The street lights come on. She gets up to draw the big heavy curtains that came from the old house. They totally eclipse the light and she stumbles to find her way to the ceiling light switch. The little dog barks. Worried.

The fine oak Grandfather clock in the hall chimes. It's 9 o'clock. Time for bed. Jack must be working nights. She is a little forgetful perhaps?

She makes her way slowly up the stairs. She bends her rheumatoid hands around the flimsy rail. The little dog follows her sombrely. The little dog reaches the landing before her and is growling in the darkness at the top of the stairs. The old lady puts on the landing light. The dog is silent.

The small child is sitting on the edge of the bed observing the old lady. When the old lady falls asleep the small child lays against her chest. She breathes in rhythm with the old lady. The breaths are long drawn and rasping. The stale oxygen in the bedroom hangs in the air unsure. The small child holds her breath... and finally.

The little dog growls anxiously in its sleep.

The small child looks at the clock on the bedroom wall. Almost midnight. She looks from above and whispers, 'Daddy, daddy, mummy is coming. She's finally coming. You can stop all your worrying'. All the clocks stop.

The little dog howls.

The Bridge

—LIAM HOGAN

The bridge was built over the delta, over the wide expanse of sluggish river. A massive steel structure from the days of the Titanic, from the days of the first skyscrapers.

From the days of a Colonial Empire keen to stamp its authority on the lands it had newly conquered.

3 miles long it stretches, a wonder of turn of the century—turn of the *last* century—engineering. The supports rest on rocky out-croppings, one-time home for gulls and terns. It bulges ponder-ously in the middle, a fat slip-road lapping at a cluster of islands and the pleasure gardens they once held, created to serve the very best to the very wealthiest of colonists.

Those islands are islands no more. The thirsty city drank the river dry. All that remains are subterranean passages that gurgle beneath busy streets, passages that clog in storms and flood the basements with garbage and sewage.

Now, the bridge arches over suburbs that swarm across reclaimed land, the two halves of the city made one, the shifting tapestry of sand and water firmly fixed. Only the existence of this ancient bridge that shares the river's forgotten name tells visitors what was once here.

Now, a sprawling shanty town nestles up to the mighty but-tresses, a solid base against which to rest their flimsy walls. The rust-mottled steel frame shelters haphazard markets and sin-gle-room schools populated by black-footed children, too old to suckle, too young to work.

The cracked roadway, high above, teems with bicycles and mopeds and the occasional tuk-tuk. The train that ran down the middle runs no longer, its rumbling passage a threat to the relic's ageing superstructure. Instead, weary foot passengers traipse over the blackened timbers, loads piled high on creaking shoulders. Stalls are set up in the thin shade of a stanchion, serving up scalding black coffees, sticky rice wrapped in lotus leaves, or evil pipes of tobacco mixed with whatever is the stimulant du-jour. Anything to keep the people moving, this daily influx of farmers, refugees, and immigrants swelling the city's already swollen ranks.

This is the flow the bridge now serves.

But the slumbering giant knows nothing of this. The bridge basks in hazy sun and dreams of water.

Grief

—CLARE PALMER

When the phone call comes, you know. You have been waiting for this day, yet hoping your son could drive the dark clutching horrors from his mind.

'My son is dead', you say. 'My son has killed himself'. You try out a new phrase, these five words that are difficult to assemble in the right order. 'My son has committed suicide.'

Your husband tells you there was nothing more you could have done. You know there will be many attempts to persuade you not to blame yourself, not to feel guilty.

Your other son, his brother, is waiting at the house. You hug him as if you could make him part of your body again, lie curled and safe in your belly. He pulls away. He needs to tell you what has happened, what will happen next. His face is drawn and aged with shock. He tells you the police do not want you to see your dead son, it would be too distressing.

The evening, the night, the next morning pass. Somewhere in that time you eat a little soup, brought by your neighbour. You sleep briefly, fitfully till you are woken by your own weeping. Your husband holds you as you shudder and gasp.

This grief is as raw and red as birth. It burns in your chest, catches the breath, rams into the solar plexus. It is hard work, it leaves you wearied and wearisome. You move like an automaton, putting one foot in front of the other as you move from front door to kitchen, from kitchen to garden. It catches you and spins you round, it makes you sit, motionless, staring at the wall opposite. You lose control of your voice, laments are keening sounds, not words.

His friends, shattered, guilt-stricken, loving, come to your house every evening. They bring photos, stories. There is laughter, too, as they remember him. They plan the funeral, choose music and poems. His wife, estranged from him since his angry despair defeated their marriage, sits next to you holding your hand tightly. Your husband makes pot after pot of food for them, makes tea, pours wine, looks after you, looks after them, keeps everyone alive.

It is as if time itself is drawn into the vortex of your son's death, is no longer in control of minutes and hours. You sit in your garden, wrapped up warmly by others. You don't know how you will make it through the next minute. And then it is an hour later. The telephone rings. You speak to the police, to the undertaker. Cards are dropped through the letterbox. There is a knock at the door and another friend arrives carrying flowers. You welcome embraces now.

You count the days since he died. Since he killed himself. Since he committed suicide. Since he died.

Soul Talking
—PAM WILLIAMS

A vague familiarity made me look twice. I scowled, embarrassed by his stare. Then ran from it; kicking a stone and chasing it down the street.

There was no escape when Mum said 'Tony, this is your father'.

And there he was. His shoes shone. Dark socks, dark trousers, muscled legs. A stomach flat and hard, beneath the heavy buckle that lay on top the slim-fitting shirt. A chin wrapped in tight black curls that grew straighter as they crawled over his top lip and up the sides of his face, then tightened again to sit low and neat on his head.

He smiled even white teeth at me and stretched out his hand. I wanted to spit in it. I don't think I'd ever spat at anyone in my life. But I wanted to. To hawk up phlegm from the back of my throat the way I'd seen boys in the playground do and lob it at him through my lips that looked too much like his.

'Go get changed. Then come back'. Mum sensed my instinct to run.

I was relieved to move away from him, so 'brand new penny' looking. Compared to my sweat-soaked, after school, kick-about self.

Faced with the reality of him I was forced to feel. But what? Happy he'd sought me out? Grateful he'd bestowed that stunning smile on me? Angry it had taken him so long to claim me? Defensive in case this was a one off?

Every weekend he showed up. His lilting voice so molten its touch began to soften me. He was careful not to hurry me, bonding with me over tales of us. As a not quite-four-year-old when he left, my unripe memory hadn't stored them. Him.

He developed a fondness for that chair in the kitchen. And mum for keeping busy. She never stopped to join the conversation, her silence implying 'it's your business not mine'. She cared though.

Time allowed my heart to crack open its door. Foolish me. I should have known better. He was ill. That's why he wanted to know me. To salve his diseased conscience.

Was this the pain I should have felt back then? The door that emotion had barely pushed ajar, closed tight.

With determined disinterest, I watched his unconscious form, tightly tucked beneath off-white sheets. Was he gone? Should I know? I avoided the eyes of the nurse who said how sad losing a father must be. She hadn't known hers. *Me neither* I wanted to mutter. My tongue stayed still. But restlessness escaped my too well-behaved for too long body. Mum led me from the inaudible crowd of strangers that surrounded his bed.

The phone disturbed dawn. Awake, I refused to move, not wanting to witness Mum's reaction. Would this final loss crumple her? Despite the years? Let her mourn, said a voice deep within my soul. The news could wait till morning, when grief could be wiped from her face and normality repainted there.

He was Brixton Blue

—ANDRÉS ORDORICA

It's ten past one on the Northern line heading south. He takes a
seat at Camden. Smiling and nodding. He's fucking drunk. But,
he likes blue eyes. The very blue of the person in front of him.
He doesn't know if he is muttering aloud or not. But, he thinks he
is responding. Yes, someone is asking him questions.

Where you off to?

Home.

Great. Good night?

Yes. Works drinks.

Piss up?

Guess so…you're very talkative!

Sorry. Didn't mean to…

No. I'm sorry. That made me sound like a prick.

A bit.

Those eyes could hold an ocean that he would spend years
sailing if he could, swimming, consuming those eyes.

The blue eyes move back and forth in a circle. He realises he
is not the only drunk heading home. Amusing to see someone try
and defy gravity.

The driver announces a breakdown. Oval station. Apologies
for any inconvenience, but fuck he has a long way to go.

Fuck.

This is shit, right?

Yes.

He gets up and exits the station. The air on the street is both
warm and damp. Summer. What to do? A bus home would be
too long for his stomach. He is too skint for an Uber. Walk home?

That seems smart.

He tries to find a street map. Where is he? Yes, Oval...there's the cricket ground. He starts to walk toward Clapham. Home isn't that far.

He feels a presence with him as he walks. Not a ghost, but a physical one. Blue eyes.

Walking home, too?

Yeah.

Fucking mental that it just broke down like that.

I guess so.

Anyway, I'm Tom.

Great...are you stalking me?

He seems shocked. Both are as the moment is ruined. He is drunk and mincing words. He does not want to be aggressive.

I am going to get going.

Sorry. It's the shots talking.

It's fine. I shouldn't have. I was just guessing.

Guessing?

He is hurt. Those blue eyes now filled with such sad beauty.

I'm Darrell.

I'm going home. Asshole.

You can walk with me.

Why bother?

Your eyes.

Excuse me?

Your eyes are wonderful. They remind me of the skies back home.

Dublin?

Your eyes are the blue of Irish summer.

...

-Okay.

Okay, what?

I'll walk with you.

What is he doing? He has never met a man before. This was

scary, but those eyes. An unreal blue entrapping him and opening up parts of him he tried so hard to quell. Cars speed on by during the deep dark of night. It's an entirely different city in the dark. He was an entirely different person.

Before he knew it, it's 'this is me.'

Well, I am still off to Clapham.

Brixton blue.

What?

You can call me that I guess.

Brixton blue it is.

He kisses him on the cheek. It pains him how much he wants more, a number or to be invited in. But, he can't allow it.

So, he keeps walking south. Smiling and wincing all the same.

Mr Pal's Retreat
—COURTTIA NEWLAND

Many years later, Mr Pal sits on the curb of Whitechapel Road, his legs wide open and his hands limp between them, staring into the gutter. Rafi sees him first. He pulls at my shoulder. I hardly recognise him, then I do.

We go over, crouching beside him. He's muttering or singing something I can't hear. His trainers are worn and black, split at the front like an open mouth. His suit, which was always neat, is torn at the left sleeve and his white shirt is black with grime, billowing in the breeze of passing traffic. We speak to him, and each other, in Bengali. I'm not sure he recognises us anymore, as there's nothing in his eyes, but he talks back in return, saying something about retreating. We don't know what he means by that. Rafi suggests we lift him. He's the oldest, and I'm used to doing what he says, so I shrug and say 'Sure.' We tell him what we're about to do and make good on our promise. He's light, all bones and cotton. It feels as though he hasn't had a good meal for months.

He leans on us all the way to his home, gives us the keys and we let him in. Going upstairs he stops and stiffens, pulling against us as if he wants to go back on the street. We resist him, and it's a tug of war until Rafi opens his flat. The stink's terrible. Old rubbish, mouldy food, unwashed old man. Mr Pal gives up then, it's almost like the smell sedates him. We lift him the rest of the way, and deposit him on the sofa. Rafi turns on the spot, looking at the wall.

'Jesus,' he says, which is unusual for my brother. He doesn't take deity's names in vain, even when they're not ours. I'm keeping an eye on Mr Pal in case he makes another break for it, so at first I don't see where he's looking. When Rafi doesn't speak again, I clock it as the second weird thing he's done in as many minutes. I check on him too, and see why.

Mr Pal didn't bring much from Bangladesh, but the thing I always remember is the photo of his mum hanging above the electric fireplace. It's pretty big, and it was actually me who helped him to frame it when we found the print amongst his things, just after I really got into photography myself. It's one of those old sepia tinted ones, and must have cost a bomb at the time. She's sitting on an unseen chair, looking into camera wearing a sari with her head covered, and it must have been taken when he was young because I have to say she looks beautiful. I dunno if it's the colour enhancement or the way she always was, because her eyes are bright hazel, and a really nice shape. They don't look alike at all, apart from something in the twist of her mouth, but Mrs Pal's smiling and Mr Pal hardly does that type of thing.

That's how it used to look anyway, has done for years. Only now, half of the photo and Mrs Pal with it have faded into some inky, black kind of fog that obscures the left side of her face, and everything else on that side with it.

Mr Pal rocks on the sofa. 'Retreating,' he says, pointing at his mum. 'All retreating.'

Rafi asks what happened, but that's all Mr Pal says. Retreating, retreating. His English had got better since we were kids, so it's a shame to see him regress to the Mr Pal we knew way back when. Rafi makes that whistle noise you use to say someone's cuckoo. I frown at him; that isn't fair. I get up to take a closer look at the photo, and there's smaller ones lining the mantel, these landscape colour snapshots like you used to get from the pharmacy. Old school. Grinning kids, an upright family, a young girl caught mid-cartwheel, kicking village dust.

Except each one's obscured by that fogged, fading blackness, like Polaroids in reverse. Instead of developing these pictures are dissolving, retracting into a misty, unreadable past.

'Retreating!' Mr Pal says, seeing my face. 'All retreating!'

He shuffles out of the room, so slow we don't stop him. The sound of rummaging comes from a back room. When he returns, Mr Pal is holding blossoming sheets of crumpled paper. He gives them all to me. They're yellowed, lined, and filled with scrawling handwriting; the ink's deep blue like sailors' tattoos. Or so it seems. When I look closer I see the writing's also fading, leaving half words and blank lines, exactly as they were before they'd been scrawled on. I look at Rafi. He gapes.

'Shit,' he says.

'Exactly!' Mr Pal screeches, laughing as if it's all a big joke.

We sit on the sofa in a row. Me, Mr Pal, and Rafi. We spread the colour photos on the coffee table together with the letters, trying to work out what's going on. Mr Pal explains in Bengali. It started happening recently, he says. First he couldn't say whether he had a grown up niece, or a nephew. Then he couldn't remember his mother's name. Then the house he was born in, or the village he grew up in, or the country he'd left to come to England. All of it had faded and retreated from him. When they'd disappeared, it began happening to the things he'd brought over from Bangladesh too.

Rafi looks at me. I look at Rafi. To be honest we don't know what to say. My bro takes Mr Pal's left hand. I take his right. He begins to cry, his thin shoulders shaking with emotion, tears collecting in the crevices of his face. All we can do is gently rub his gnarled, stiffened fingers. We lie, and tell him everything's OK.

Wise Owl! Eyes Like A Hawk

—DANIELLE HIGGINS

Through my huge dark round eyes I kept wistful watch over the wood each and every night. While the others slept softly snoozing under the bright yellow crescent moon I kept lookout.

It was in late November when a poacher man dressed in rags with a basket, stick and hook stumbled upon our neck of the woods. At first he would forage in the light of day for wild mushrooms, plums, berries and cob nuts in small quantities, but his hunger grew. Every night geese squawking in trauma would flap frantically until his haunting hook broke some poor souls neck. While, whole communities of rabbits were captured in the cruellest of ways and left to suffer slow undignified deaths. Even the crayfish in the river, and our eggs—all gone! Our community had never witnessed such carnage, and I could do nothing. I helplessly watched on and recorded what I witnessed night after night. Hopelessly, I hung my head to the leaf covered ground and wept relentlessly.

On my panic stricken travels to find a solution I floundered past some fellow citizens flying freely, and in passing conversation we set out to stop the poacher whom had made our lives so unbearable. Our plan would be unstoppable. Unbreakable! We waited and watched and waited some more… Only the moonlight flickered on the rivers water and everything calm. Like clockwork the poacher came bound dutifully as a creature of habit.

I found my position and flew flapping frantically at his head. He cried out in pain as my claws scratched at his spineless head. Then what sounded like a choir of angels that came to my rescue; a multitude of beautiful birds sang as loud as could be.

Tu-we, to-witta-woo, zzzzzd and clack clack clack, the wood was filled with all manner of amazing sounds. The hungry sparrow-hawk swept into the poacher pecking at his eyes and fingers. The shrills became alarming. As more birds heard, the more joined in on the crazy frenzy, and the kestrel swooped in and clawed at his cheek. The poacher, bleeding and traumatized, fled swiftly back over his tracks sometimes stumbling in the dark. His silhouetted figure bent doubled and visibly crippled with pain.

As the events of the evening settled I took stand on my post, and wide awake watched the wild and green wood in its richness and splendour. The calm river shimmering under the soft light of the moon. Where blurred black bats are glimpsed and gone. How the sweet calls and tunes of birds sing themselves to sleep. These melodies hummed in celebration of the start of my watch. Lord and master of all I survey; for now and all of the night hours these huge big eyes will watch over the wood. Woe betides who trespasses here and unsettles my watch!

The Crow
—ANNA LATIMER

She scooped him up from the wet tarmac, out of the paths of dogs and joggers and the buggies, where babies rode high, like royalty, amidst their canopies of colour. He was unsteady on his feet, hobbling drunkenly, unformed and vulnerable to foxes and stalking cats. She folded him tenderly into her scarf, holding his trembling body close, feeling the spring of his legs, the frantic scratching of his claws. Guiltily, on the bus, she kept him hidden under the shelter of her coat, until reaching home she released him onto the kitchen floor where he fixed her with his blue eye and opened his beak wide.

He forced her into foreign territory, into the earth where the grubs and worms lived their hidden lives. Mercilessly she cut them into pieces and holding his beak open pushed them to the back of his throat so that he gulped and swallowed. He learned to follow her, hopping from room to room. He mirrored back her voice, whilst she learned to echo his harsh 'caw, caw.' His feathers became sleek and black. In the evenings he met her at the door, settled himself upon her shoulder and nibbled at her pale ear. In the dark of the night he grew tall and perched himself amongst the branches of his wish fulfilling tree whilst her wings grew. Together, they spiralled up above the city and kept watch over the glittering night.

Tommy's Snake Tattoo
—JON FORTGANG

Tommy didn't strike you as a man interested in body art. Solid. Balding. Fifty-ish. He never said very much yet somehow knew the answer to everything: how to re-balance a crankshaft; the name of the Egyptian god of the Sun.

Tommy was a driver. I was Tommy's mate. We delivered fridges in south-west London. I was eighteen. This was '97. The year I lost my dad. I told Tommy all about that. More, probably, than he wanted to know. Two men in a tail-lift Luton—one of 'em's going to talk. But Tommy listened and nodded sadly, steering us round Richmond with the Hotpoints in the back.

Summer came and Tommy rolled up his sleeves revealing that tattoo. It coiled around his forearm. The mouth encircled his wrist. It looked recent. I was impressed. I'd been thinking about getting something myself. But I wondered what it meant. Artwork like that, on a man like him. I couldn't reconcile it. I asked Tommy but he shrugged.

'Everyone looks for meaning.' We were in Brentford. 'But some things have no meaning at all.' He sounded sad. Tommy often did. But the sadness was like a suburb beyond which lay a wilderness you couldn't map. That was how it seemed. He lifted his arm and looked at the tattoo, almost as if it wasn't part of him. We drove on silently to Kew.

In August I went on holiday. Two weeks in Ibiza. I wanted to remember my dad. But mostly I wanted to forget. On my first day back Les the gaffer approached me.

'What's that?' he said.

'What's what?'

'That.' He gestured at my arm.

'Tattoo.'

'It's Tommy's tattoo,' said Les. 'Isn't it?'

And okay. It kind of was. I'd sketched it from memory one night while having an imaginary conversation with my dad. By the time the tequilas came my dad had been replaced by Tommy. Next day I'd had it done. It was meant to be a tribute. Now I wasn't sure.

'You know what that tattoo means?' said Les.

'Everyone looks for meaning.' I said. 'But…'

'To Tommy. What it means to Tommy?'

'No.'

'That's the tattoo his lad had.'

This was news to me. 'Tommy's… got a son?'

'Not anymore,' said Les. 'Motorbike accident. Last summer. Stu had that snake on his arm. Then Tommy got it himself. To keep a bit of Stu alive.' Les looked at me. 'You didn't know that?'

'No.'

Les sighed. 'You do now.'

At the start of the shift Tommy was already in the van. I climbed in and when he clocked the snake he visibly recoiled. But he didn't say anything at all. We sat together in silence: me without my father, him without his son. There's some skin you just can't shed. Tommy rolled his sleeve down, concealing the tattoo. I looked across at him and it was as if there was a vast space between us, a wilderness you couldn't map. I got out and left him there.

Watch and Wait
—RUTH GOLDSMITH

It's already 9.13 PM. She's late. Later than usual.

Dusk is suspended over the five tower blocks which make up the estate where she lives. From my vantage point, on the bench by the scrappy play area, I watch.

I watch as the five towers jag upwards. They're straining heroically against the sky as if trying to stop the sun from touching down. They'll lose, as they lose every night. Every night these five towers make their stand. But the dark slides down their flanks, casting shadows, trickling through windows, teasing the streetlights until they tolerate it no more and flicker on.

Forgive me. Waiting does this to a person.

There goes the first streetlight now: guttering and thrumming into sodium glow. I shift my weight, try to relax into the bench. Pour myself a few mouthfuls of lukewarm tea from my flask. I've not had to wait this long before.

Observation has been under way for seven weeks now. After thorough research, I've decided that this bench is the best spot. Not too close. Close enough.

From here, you see, I can watch as she turns the corner from the High Road. She'll have slowly climbed up the stairs out of the tube station a few minutes before. I can watch as she makes her way across the asphalt that serves as a car park, passing between two towers, before approaching the third. I can watch as she reaches into her bag, pulls out her keys. I can even watch as she places the fob on the pad next to the door and pushes, her head bowed, putting her weight into it. If the wind's right, and the sirens still for just a moment, I can hear the click as the door shuts behind her.

It's a good job the lift works. The birth certificate says she's nearly sixty. Once she's in, it doesn't take long for her to get to her flat. Number 124: the fourth flat on the twelfth floor. With the copies I made of the estate building plans at the archives, I can see that she has one bedroom, one bathroom and a south facing living room. Big windows looking out over the city. Lovely and airy, it must be.

It won't be long until I make my move. After all these years, it has to be right though. Everything could be ruined otherwise. I want her to invite me in. I want to sit across from her, at her kitchen table perhaps, or in the lounge that overlooks this park, this bench, and have a cup of tea. I want to talk about the pictures on her walls, compliment her furnishings. Tell her about myself. Ask about her life. If she ever thought of me. The adoption papers say she gave me up willingly, you see. But ever since I had my own kids, I've known that can't be true. Not really. So, I watch and wait. Until the right moment comes.

Marseille Eats Toast for Dinner
—LAUREN MILLER

Marseille eats toast for dinner.

As day bleeds into night, Marseille keeps running. Sourcing and buying painstaking ingredients, to chop, boil, mix, sizzle in some quiet kitchen are the kinds of things Marseille has no time for. Instead it craves the taste of exhaustion and sweat on its lips. Even the thought of settling down for a solitary moment, inside the cool thick stone walls of home, shutters pulled and beating out the scrambling city, makes Marseille quiver with impatience.

Marseille treasures the lilac and mauve rings under its eyes, needing sleep, too dazzled by the world to miss any of it. Marseille believes sleep is for people who don't love life enough to witness it.

If hunger pains Marseille too much, it's a store, some bread, a toaster in the corner of a crumb covered surface. Push the slices in, turn on red and go back to whatever was distracting it before; running bare-chested down alleys splintered with sunlight, staring in awe at the beauty of the women who stand in the doorways of the houses that curve uphill, old wooden chairs sitting beside them empty, laughing in the face of the glittering riches that occupy themselves around the harbour, out of the way of the real life.

The moment after the toast jolts up, only then does Marseille allow itself to breathe. The smell of the burnt bread is too charred for most people to bother with. But Marseille has to bother with it, there's no time to go through it all again.

The night voices are stirring outside, calling too Marseille through the dust covered window, wide open so as never to be separated from the city smells. It grabs the toast with pincer fingers, burnt edges singeing its fingertips. No plate, no need. Marseille bites one slice down in four mouthfuls, on its way out the door, mouth full to forget the loneliness.

Out on the street the sky is ink but the silver burns, like sun when it catches the crests of breaking waves, still drives the scruffy city through the neo-byzantine facades and the night, into the day, then all over again.

Warrier of the No. 68

—KATHERINE DAVEY

The girl sat at the back of the number 68 from Euston. She imagined she had bow, with the string tightly drawn. Like the girl from the Hunger Games. Except here, on the number 68. There'd be no one on the top deck. She'd open the small window that lifts, lengthways, and she'd aim at something. Someone. Someone bad. Though she hadn't thought that part through—how she'd know how bad they really were. But she'd aim at something moving, which would be a person most likely, because from the top deck a cat or a dog would be difficult—too small—and cats, particularly, too slippery in their movement. The eels of the pavements. And cats and dogs weren't ever bad. So, a person. Maybe on a bike, or pushing a buggy, or something that kept them on a steady line so that she could move the point of her arrow just a little ahead, knowing they'd be likely to move into the line of it. That's what they did. On films and in the Olympics. Or clay pigeon shooting, or duck shooting. All of that. A man on a bike screaming at a girl to fucking get out of the way. A woman talking on her phone rather than to her crying child, or slapping it and yelling and telling it to shut up. She'd aim for the chest, so she'd have to make sure the bus was on the route up Pentonville Road, going up, with her on the top deck on the right side, and the people coming down the other side, so that she'd have a clear view and aim over the oncoming traffic, or the gaps in it. It'd be no good trying to get the arrows to angle down on the pavement side from the top deck. The windows were too narrow, and she'd have the movement of the bow. And then when she had it just right, a clear view, and the string taut, she'd simply part her finger and thumb, as if she were dropping a marble and gravity were taking it cleanly away.

And someone would be dead. The amazing thing about it all would be how peculiar it would be to have done it. And then still to be on the 68 going along. Because she bets the driver wouldn't notice a thing. They never notice much—specially not when you're trying to flag them down before they pull away, and you're still running up the pavement trying to catch them. They manage never to notice that. So she doesn't except they'd have their eyes peeled for some person shot swiftly with an arrow. She's not sure what she'd do next, though. It's one of those things. It's all very well but you have to come back to reality at some point. Like reading romantic fiction. There's normal life on either side of it. So perhaps she wouldn't do that, after all.

The Death of Old Raffy
—JOSEPHINE PHILLIPS

A hub of life, stretching half a mile, from Barking Road through to Hallesville Road. Stalls and shops for one and all, from carpets and haberdashery to live chickens. From pie and mash and jellied eels to a glass of sarsparilla. and a pub or two. Crammed with kids, prams, mums and dads, buying and selling or just looking, this was old 'Raffy'.

Regeneration, we here call, and new homes promised too. Em but this meant the end of old 'Raffy" as we knew it! What was left of it, emerged on the Barking Road sandwiched between Caters, the new fangled Supermarket in town and the Ordnance Arms. We had some of the good old traders back, Thakes the Fishmonger, Jollys the Greengrocers. Pollards for all things household and ladies tights and Unique Stores for your glass, china and giftware. Regeneration we heard called again, 'what we cry'? When this new 'Raffy' was blitzed and replaced by high rise apartments, a few for rent but mostly to buy at extortionate money. They cleansed the 'Towners' pushing us out far and wide, to Essex and beyond, anywhere but old 'Raffy', Canning Town. Land values had escalated, aided and abetted by the coming of the Jubilee Line, The Olympic Legacy the DLR and Crossrail coming in quick pursuit, giving instant and speedy access to the City and City wages and beyond—like China.

The flats, high rise, middle rise, state of the art and some just a state are all flying up two a penny. Tomorrow's slums. All made out of ticky tacky and all just the same. Forget that the 22 Storey Ronan Point blew up and the rest were knocked down with the exception of Ferrier Point—to be refurbished to a high spec and sold off! Now refurbed at some exorbitant cost has social housing and children on the 18th floor! Now we have more pollution than in decades, children with allergies and asthma. Now we've got the good old takeaway food packaging littering the streets; forage for the ravaging rats and foxes! Plastic bottles strewn everywhere, no more penny on return! Pavements new or old, speckled with chewing gum waiting for the rain to do its best to clean some of it up. Every bus stop, railway station and shopping area strewn with cigarette butts. Parks full of dog poo, bins too few, people with no bags and no brains. A council only interested in fining people rather than dealing with the causes. Homes fit for purpose got knocked down for the value of the land, social engineering at its finest, replaced by regen/trification. Fortunately we still have scraps of good community, a thriving Library, home to Rathbone Writers and more story telling, what remains of the market and the wonderful school choirs. Look how great it could be if we stopped building ugly high rises.

It's all about the money, money, money, it's all about the money!

The Watcher
—JULIE BROWNE

I've been waiting all this time, watching for the sign. The message the enemy has been defeated and He is on his way back. Please gods let this be over soon. I can't take much more of being in limbo, not knowing what is going to become of us. I can't see in the stars what our future will be. I can't sleep, I can't feel pleasure or ease until I know what happens so my watch can be over.

I am sitting on a concrete step by the side of the Thames near Tower Bridge. Watching a free play outdoors. It's a warm summer evening, the lights are flickering along the bridge, torches light up the amphitheatre. The Oresteia. I vaguely know that it is ancient Greek, not more. I am here purely because it is free and the evening is too pleasant to want to go home to my sweat box little flat.

I am not prepared for the seismic shift about to happen. Sitting outside, watching a play about a Greek Hero coming back from Troy and a Greek Heroine avenging the murder of her daughter and the insult to her home, the place she has governed while He was away fighting and whoring, feasting and drinking, dragging back the spoils of his war, gold and exotic women.

I feel a shiver, I am in a Time machine. I am in Athens, seated on a stone bench on a warm summer evening, listening to the cicadas, smelling the wild thyme, seeing the actors in their masks declaiming on the stage, the Chorus chanting their lines. I have cheese, bread and wine, and a folded blanket to sit on and I am transfixed by the tragedy unfolding in front of me.

Now I understand everything, this world of naked male privilege, before Christianity. Women are just the furrow men plough and plant their seed in, just vessels. So of course a father is more important than a mother. Women from these ancient times speak to me, about their lives of spinning, weaving, the home and children, or as sex slaves, objects taken in war, their powerlessness in the face of male power and abuse. And how they are punished by death if they try to change this script. So they just had to wait like that watchman to see what their fate would be.

I can make more sense of my life, of its possibilities and limits. Just like this play, this world was never meant for me. I shouldn't be seeing this. I can't believe it has taken me so long to get to this. I spent most of my life thirsting for things I wasn't supposed to have. But here I am gorging on violence, death, revenge, and the fickleness of the gods.

And look!

The beacon is lit. The enemy vanquished. Now I decide what happens.

Devil's in the Detail
—SAUNDRA DANIEL

He never studied the psychology of clothes. There must be a study on clothes. The fascinating thing about clothes is that they make you move a certain way, some encouraging pronounced deportment or bringing an aura, affecting the whole being. People were fickle though, making lazy assumptions because of the clothes you wear, or how you presented, deciding what you have or haven't got.

It must be part of that seven plus minus two, bits of information that people can take in at any one time. It had helped him, he wasn't complaining. Well timed patter, misdirection, sleight of mouth, especially when people were in their own self-induced hypnosis, somnambulistic through conversations of their own minds.

His favourite study on power was the obedience to authority, *The Milgram Experiment*; and his presence, gave the air of authority.

Confidence. *Watch your thoughts; they become words.* The difference between him and others was that he was confident. *Watch your words; they become actions.* He loved that word, confidence. *Watch your habits; they become character.* Confidence man. *Watch your character; it becomes your destiny.* Were those *Lao Tzu's* words?

He brushed the feather from his shoulder, like he saw his estranged son do in some dance. Duck feathers got everywhere, or maybe it was an angel. He flicked the stubborn reminder away. Last night had gone by in a flash; she was accommodating in every way, her deep sleep an abreaction from ventures in the shower, kitchen and bedroom.

He obviously left before she woke, he won't see her again.

He reassured himself that her credit card was in his pocket and contemplated the clean streets ahead, far from the days when he would play hopscotch to avoid the dog shit on his way to school. Instead, he could now use his height more effectively and keep his watchful eyes on more important things and allow them to skilfully dart in the periphery behind his Oakley's, whilst his face pointed down on her phone. It was all about timing.

'Hey Phil. Phil!'

The Newsagent was calling out to him. He smiled and entered.

'How's business? Here's a Redbull on the house'.

'Thanks Dave.' Always important to remember a person's name, it's the sweetest sound—in any language; Dale Carnegie, that's why he used her name repeatedly last night. 'About your son, Jake, I'll see if we can get a position for him, he's a good lad.' Phil, watched as the slow-witted youngster unloaded stock from the back of the shop.

'Phil, where did you say you worked again?' Newsagents had a knack for serving customers three at a time: ears, arms, eyes; their talents were wasted.

'Can see you're busy Dave, see you in the morning.' He picked up The Times and Dave nodded acceptance for him to take it for free.

Oxford Street was crowded, crowded meant busy, busy meant profit. He has had his eyes on some Ozwald Boateng collections.

He buttoned his jacket, it was time to go to work.

Acropolypse
—ANNA JAMES

It began with the gargoyles. Later, when much of London lay in ruins, this was forgotten. Much easier to believe the official version: that a clock-tuner, employed to tweak the chimes of Big Ben (the dings being a little off-key), tampered instead with the dongs. So that at one o'clock on the day now known as Acropolypse, Big Ben kept on chiming—dong, dong, dong, dong... thirteen times. And so the inevitable happened. Big Ben chimes thirteen times: the lions in Trafalgar Square come to life. It's a longstanding myth: traditional, popular—indeed, almost plausible—were it not so patently false.

Of all the many metamorphoses that happened that day, the first was a small, griffinish gargoyle perched on the tower of St. Mary's in Acton. The how or the why isn't for here—what I want you to picture is the gargoyle's expression as it was suddenly transformed from cold stone into a living, creaturely thing. With a mute screech it opened its beak, stiff from snarling so long. Below in the market-place, sellers cried out their wares. The gargoyle gazed down at the flashing neon of a nail salon and a 99p store. A gaggle of teenagers spilled from Chicken Cottage, threw chips at each other and slouched up the road back to school. The gargoyle uncoiled its tail and flexed its long lion's claws. People in the market looked up as it shook lichen and moss from its scales. And that was the first of the sightings—just gone midday—as the gargoyle unfurled its stubby, stone wings and hurled itself up over Morrisons' roof.

Many more gargoyles followed. From Shepherd's Bush to St. Pancras, Pimlico to the Isle of Dogs, parapets stood empty, the strange, unholy creatures that had gurned and grimaced there for centuries now circling high overhead. Detached from their guttering, no longer mere rain-spouts, they were free to delight in their own gruesomeness. Whether feathered or scaly, leonine, dog-faced or troglodytic, they all swooped and screeched with unmistakable glee.

It wasn't long before the angels joined in. From tombs and monuments all over London, heavenly hosts rose, spread their soft marble wings and merged with the demonic rabble above. Irrespective of hierarchy they thronged—angels and archangels, seraphim and cherubim—some strumming harps, others tossing their haloes like hoopla over the Shard.

Naturally, other effigies soon followed suit. A good ten minutes before Big Ben's thirteen dongs, Lord Nelson was cowering on top of his column, bird droppings dripping like sweat. Below him, four huge lions stalked the square as tourists stampeded away. It was the same scene on the Embankment: the sphinxes at Cleopatra's Needle yawned and wriggled their haunches, preparing to rampage, as panicked office workers dropped their sandwiches and threw themselves into the Thames.

By the time the thirteenth dong had reverberated over London, snipers were already in place, fighter jets had been scrambled, and all sorts of sculpture was winging its way overhead.

Britain Lost and Found

—HARVINELL TATTON

If Britain was a book it would be bought by an American million-aire with a yearning for nostalgia.

The lettering on its pages would be an eclectic mix of old-fashioned calligraphy and modern dynamic typography laid on a background of cream linen paper. The inner spine would be held by handmade ridges to ensure longevity and future profitability.

Verses from the Bible and Shakespeare would spiral down its spine to create an outer backbone: a celebration of their combined influences on British law, culture, and liberty. The edges of its pages would be a sparkling sky blue, stamped with pictures taken from around the British coastline, a celebration of its island shape. There would be quirky touches, like a pop-up flag of Great Britain, jigsaw-style at the very centre.

The American would love its content: the varied snapshots of British life, from the medieval to the modern. Delighting in a history shared through artistry, personal stories, drawings, poems, recipes and of course, photography. Each strand reflecting the cultural diversity of the land. He would mark the blank diary pages at the end, inviting personal anecdotes and secret wishes for enjoying life under the umbrella of 'Britain'.

The American businessman would enjoy 'Britain' until one day he left the world for pastures new. A public trust would then buy back 'Britain 'and give it a new title namely: *Britain Lost and Found: Collected Historical and Modern Experiences of Living in Britain*. The new owners would put 'Britain' on display in a public gallery for all to see as a gift to the community.

The profit would come from the merchandising, which would prove a touch enterprising. The gallery bookshop would sell pocket-sized editions of the book, with an invitation to 'join the next big read', marketing cute jigsaw boxes containing the flag in 'Britain'. For the artistic, the range would include a sketch book with a selection of pre-drawn images of the British coastline. For thirsty, hungry visitors, the gallery café would serve miniature cake versions of 'Britain' with afternoon tea. The top would be an iced front cover of the book. And hidden underneath?—a regional treat from its chapter of recipes. All served of course, on fine Royal Dalton china, on a bed of white paper doilies.

Sales would begin as a trickle then become a growing tide with many owning a copy, adding to their own surprise a personal chapter to the contents of *'Britain Lost and Found.'* Thus, accidentally creating an expanded edition of the book.

And later in the gallery their anecdotes of experience and hope, would be exhibited, embraced and celebrated as a communal triumph of domestic and international bonding. Not unlike the works on display in 1851 at Crystal Palace.

The new public would be ignited with Victorian earnestness, but without the pomp and circumstance. Then 'Britain' would breathe as a living book not just a written book.

Living

—CLAIRE BAKER

1960

Farewell my love. The dark hole in my soul is a raw pulsating thing. My heart is shredded. Torn to searing pieces. I lay dry eyed on the freshly laid mound. Hoping that its cold crumbling surface would suddenly warm to my touch; bringing you back to me. How can I say goodbye?

1961

I have been dreading this day. It feels like the past year has been an achingly slow countdown towards this moment. Treading through one dark, cold day after another. Pretending to eat, sleep, smile. I look at the mound, now freshly laid with frail spikes of green. It feels so cruel that such small things continue to grow without you in the world. The earth beneath my fingers is still cold, but firm. Like it belongs there now. My heart squeezes. I am surprised. My shredded heart has not disintegrated after all.

1962

Today I ache. Is it me or has the mound grown smaller? The tufts of green sprout sturdily, proprietorially beneath my fingers. 'I miss you.' The words come silently from my soul. A solitary tear rolls down one bare cheek. I realise I have accepted you are gone. The tear turns into a heaving, snotty flood. I feel like I am drowning in a well of sadness I can never break free from.

Summer 1962

There is someone with me. We stand silently. I concentrate on breathing. The clamour of words in my head turn into a few whispered sounds. It helps, Sal says, to chat like she is still with me. Sal is right. There are tears but I am not the broken snivelling wreck she found two months ago.

Winter 1962

This is my tenth visit this year. The trees, normally studded with unfurling green spikes, are lean skeletons rattling in the wind. We talk, the mound an icy cushion beneath my coat. I apologise for not coming sooner at this time of year, to relieve the grey with a few sprays of flowers and titbits of gossip from my ordinary life.

1963

I am a changed man. Or so I fancy. The day has dawned cool and overcast. The white clouds flood everything with a clinical light. Today no longer fills me with fear, nor incapacitates me with sorrow. Sal's support group has helped. She is waiting for me now. I smile and wave. Then give a tea shaped lift of my fingers. She nods. Our steps fall in sync with each other. I am starting to feel whole.

I Can't Look

—VICTORIA TAYLOR

I'm standing outside our old front door. I can't look behind me because that would mean I see you. But then you are everywhere here in my childhood home, my childhood street.

Let's look across the road first, to the little church. Thankfully they only ring their bells on special occasions, so I don't mind that. You only took me inside its boring concrete walls once, a summer fete I think it was. Apart from the small bell tower, it didn't even look like a church, it blended well with the long monotonous houses that ran the length of the 'other' side.

Our side of the road was much more exciting. You grab my hand and I can't resist the flow of pleasure that that causes. I don't often get to hold your hand, you are usually pushing the double buggy with your small charges. I didn't begrudge them your love, at the end of the day they went home and then you were all mine.

Our neighbour, as always, waved to me from the counter of his sweet shop and you pull along as I try to head in his direction. We reach the first corner and I wince as I remember going over the handlebars of my bike, right there where the concrete is buckled and broken.

From this corner our street really opens up. To the right are three tower blocks and opposite is the Duke of Cambridge, outside are groups of old men having a natter. Beside the pub is our destination, the petrol station where we are heading to buy some milk. I start to look up at you, but no, I can't, not yet.

My thoughts drag me now to my last childhood home. This house and street are so different. No shops, flats or petrol stations here. Instead, two long rows of houses with owner's cars fighting for position outside. Four bedrooms now and two large reception rooms, but the double buggy remains.

It was from this house that I got my first job, first boyfriend and eventually left to get married. In this house you hugged me with joy as I showed you my ultrasound picture. That double buggy was used when you looked after my son so I could go back to work. I couldn't have done that if it wasn't you that was holding him instead of me.

This house was also the one I moved back into when the cough that you kept shrugging off wouldn't go away. Our positions became reversed, it was now my turn to hold your hand, it was my turn to wipe the tears and hold you through the night time terrors.

When we knew we were losing you, the community knew too. So many of those babies, now grown adults came to say goodbye. They never forgot you.

I can look at you now, I can look into your eyes. I embrace the pain and there you are.

Hi mum.

Timings in a City
—CLARE VASILJEVIC

Jon woke alone, without an alarm, at six. He put on his clothes that were hanging on the door of the wardrobe. He drank coffee with toast, burnt on one side. A man in his seventies, he had never gotten use to taking care of himself. He took the underground six stops west changed and took six stops East. The day smelt that it would be hot, an empty sky with a frail breeze that would die before lunch.

He met the others at the ticket gates. They exchanged their various tribulations or ease of journeys as people invariably do when they have reached a unfamiliar destination, the person travelling the furthest gaining the most awe. Then a quick remark on the 'beautiful weather' and then the balancing 'but it's too hot.'

They moved outside into the shade, a few feet away from the transport police who were setting up camp: a metal detector through which selected young men would walk. The metal detector would be fully operational by 9.30 AM when all decent law abiding citizens under the age of 60 were already safely at work. Though, not of course an offence in itself; a citizen can walk anywhere at any time, in any style. Still certain styles and bearings are bound to raise trained suspicions.

The male and female officer exchanged the same pleasantries. The male officer then discharged himself to buy the coffees with the same zeal for hot beverages as officials everywhere. The officers gave out safety cards to the passengers and 'kept an eye out' for an individual attired and carrying themselves in a manner of being rich enough not to be rushing towards a boss but impoverished enough not to possess their own transportation.

The suspect would be indicated by a nod of the head and the affirmative nod back, a officer at either elbow. 'Sir please step this way.' The suspect would empty his pockets onto the foldable table. Like in an airport. He would either be able to travel or not be able to travel.

The station forecourt tasted of neglect, cigarettes and fast food. Jon and the others handed out cards printed: *Mind the God gap.*

'Good morning' Jon would begin as he distributed the cards. 'Where is your journey taking you?'

Mostly he was ignored sometimes the response was materialist 'Kingscross' 'To put food on the table' very occasionally idealist 'Toward my fate'. At 9.32 a young man in a baseball cap pulled out his earphones.

'Where am I going?- Towards death like the rest of us. Sooner or later.'

'Ah, yes,' Jon replied. 'So then what matters in between here, where we are now, and there?'

'I'm not sure how or if it matters,' the young man sighed. 'I just know I have to try and use it the best I can.'

'My wife finished her journey last week.'

Moved, the young man responded. 'It seems her life mattered to you.'

The old man smiled and nodded.

The young man nodded and smiled back. 'Beautiful day for it.' He said in conclusion.

'Thank you.'

The young man still smiling musingly walked on, his earphones buzzing around his neck. Where in the station he was stopped and detained for a yet unknown or pre-determined period.

Harry

—SHARON OUTTEN

It had seemed like any other day to the little Staffordshire bull ter-
rier until his owner took him to St James' Park. It was a place that
he did not know. The little dog sniffed the air that was permeated
with the smell of new mown grass. His owner stopped and tied
his lead to the railings that surrounded the ornamental lake and
ran off. The little dog whined and tried to pull free to follow him.

'What's up, mate,' a shabbily dressed young man said, approaching him and stroking the animal's head, 'looks like you're
homeless now, just like me. Perhaps we should team up. I'm
Andrew and I think I'll call you Harry.'

Andrew untied the dog's lead and for the next two years they
were inseparable. During the day they would beg in the streets
so they could afford to eat. They did quite well with Harry performing some simple tricks that Andrew had taught him. When
he sat up in the begging position or waved his forepaw beseech-
ingly at passersby he tugged at their heartstrings and they gave
generously. In the evening Harry would watch over Andrew while
he slept to protect him from anyone who would steal his meagre
possessions or beat him up for sport.

The winter set in and the weather took a turn for the worse.
Andrew had contracted a chest infection. Sleeping rough did not
help his condition but Andrew would not consider sleeping in
a shelter because they would not let him take Harry in with him.
That night they slept in an alley in Soho amid the garbage cans.
They did not let the stench bother them as it was sheltered from
the worst of the wind and rain. Harry woke up the next morning
and licked Andrew's cold face but got no response. Andrew had

died in his sleep from pneumonia. The little dog began to bark hysterically. A working girl came over to see what was going on and called for an ambulance on her mobile.

The ambulance came quickly and the paramedics loaded Andrew's remains into a body bag and onto the vehicle. Harry tried to stop them taking his beloved master away. He barked and growled at the men but his protest was met with a swift kick in his ribs causing him searing pain and sending him sprawling. Harry howled with his loss and the pain in his side. He went to chase after the ambulance as it pulled away. Harry did not see the car coming up behind him and it hit him killing him instantaneously.

Harry found himself looking around. He saw his broken little body lying in the gutter amongst the litter.

'Harry, mate, it's me,' a familiar voice called, 'come on, we're going on a big adventure.'

The little dog looked up and saw Andrew. Harry wagged his tail and ran to him. Together they entered a brilliant white light and went on to the hereafter—together forever.

One for Sorrow
—JANET POAROS

The Magpie flew down, landed on the table uninvited. He preened his feathers, then satisfied, cocked his head on one side, and surveyed the situation: wondering what he could add to his collection of sparkly, shiny things.

He had taken the bright dream. The house in the countryside, with its wonderful view across parched fields to the brilliant, king-fisher blue, Mediterranean sea. Taken too, the fragrant smell of orange and lemon trees in blossom, of bright orange and yellow fruits freshly picked. For the house was to have been built close to the edge of the citrus groves. Stolen too were the dates of warm sunshine and nights dark under a twinkling sky filled with stars.

Magpie was not content, he wanted more: and so he had returned many years later. This time he came like a thief in the night, to steal a more precious, unique thing. It was her only love, lasting and true. He must have it for himself, this lovely, vibrant being. So he took it slowly, by stealth, until only a shadow was left. Unable to stop, Magpie swooped and took that too. Now she sat alone at the table, unseeing, uncaring. The Magpie returned one more time. He saw the jug of flowers, it held no charm for him, for he could see it meant nothing at all to the woman, who sat still, cold, like a statue. He flew off to search for other more sparkling treasures.

Almost mindlessly, reluctantly the woman reached out, touched the strong leaves, then the velvety petals. It was a new, unknown experience. The beauty surprised her. She felt a soft-ness, a warmth, then a rush of love.

Love engulfed her, as she held her first granddaughter in her arms for the very first time. A bright flower. Hannah. Flower.

Later, much later she took a bloom from the jug, she studied and explored the strange and wondrous sights it held and revealed. Hannah, Japanese, meaning flower. Japan—she travelled it length and breadth. Tasted its fruits, smelled its perfumes, felt at peace: and was no longer afraid to dream. To look. To seek a new dream.

Returning to the table, where the jug still stood, she saw for the first time the true identity of the flowers. She felt the passion of Andalusia, of Flamenco coursing through veins. Her heart soared and lifted as the rhythm of guitars and castanets intensified, filling her head. Life and death, and beauty held together in one glorious, exquisite bloom—*Passiflora incarnata.*

Standing Up
—MARY JUPP

Dozing, I hear a kid crying. So I'm awake and I see a guy standing a couple of feet away up the bus aisle. He's skull faced and wearing a Nasty party tee. He's pulling at the kid's hat, laughing at him. Mean. Loud. More the kid cries, louder him laugh. And no one take no notice. I swear some people is turning away.

'Hey, man, enough.' I say, quietly but loud enough for him to hear.

Nasty blanks me and carry on.

Louder. 'Enough.'

He swings round, his face pushing forward towards mine.

'Whussat? You got summat to say old man?'

'Just leave off.'

'Fucking make me.'

Please, I so fucking want to make him; nothing will give me more pleasure. I want to stand up, grab him by his shirt, lift his feet off the floor, and drop him down the bus stairwell. Leaning over I would then shout down 'Are you alright man? Sorry about that, my hand slipped.'

I'm a big, tall motherfucker and I don't want to light up this scene any more than it's lit. So I stay seated. The mother turns round and looks at me, a worried, tight face. The kid struggles off her lap and Nasty pushes him over onto his back. Kid screams. The mother leans forward into the aisle to grab him but Nasty gets between them. And then I stand up. Stand up sounds like I go from seated to upright in one move but in reality it's more like a big black sail unfurling. Sound impressive? But it moves everything up a notch. Nasty's face travels with mine as I rise and I smell his breath, man so bad it could have melt glass.

He quickly lifts the front of his shirt, his hand move. I catch a glimpse of a knife. *Shit.* And even quicker, I feel a dull thud against my thigh, a warm trickle down my leg. He come at me again, higher this time. I raise my arm. He slashes me and this time I feel the pain.

'Holy fuck...'

The woman next to me starts to scream. Or maybe it's me. I fall back onto the seat and everything go black.

I dozing. But things, they different. Shouting, sirens and flashing lights. And someone is trying to stick something into my arm. I struggle back to reality. Realise I am in an ambulance and a paramedic is setting up an IV tube.

First thought—is she ok? Second thought I wonder... how they get me down them stairs? My third thought—I dying? And where the hell are my trousers?

A commotion going on by the ambulance door. Lifting up, I see a worried face peer in, the kid asleep on her shoulder.

'Thank you.' she mouths and smiles. Nice. I smile back. Yeah, man. The lady paramedic gently turns her away. I sink back on the stretcher. I ain't gonna die. Not here. Not now.

On the Shelf
—TONY CLELFORD

As a child, all the books in the library had been familiar or friends just waiting to be met. Now the bookshelves had been pushed so their backs were to the wall. Fewer books. Signs saying 'E-books available', 'Computers upstairs', 'Private study' and as much self-service as Sainsburys.

He fled to the nearest bookshelf for reassurance. Art & Design. What a place to end up.

'The New Brutalism.' He wouldn't find a friend there would he?

'The Corpse In 19th Century Painting.' Perhaps the purchasing librarian had felt lost like him.

He searched for Fiction. Where was Jeffrey Archer when you needed him?

And as he looked he saw her.

She was taking notes in a black A6 notebook. He was far enough away to see under the table, glimpse knees beaming white through the slashes in her black jeans. Ankle length black DMs. Black vest. Long blonde hair, real he thought, not bleached. Even from that distance he thought: God, she's nice.

He strolled over and carelessly sat at her table. He tilted his head to read the spine of the book she'd been studying.

'Living Canvas: Decorations On The Human Body'

An art student?

She looked up and caught him hunched, head lurched to one side, peering.

'Sorry.' He straightened up, thinking fast. 'I've got tattoos,' he lied.

Cool, she eyed him up and down.

'In places you can't see,' he added hastily.

No, that made things worse. She rolled her eyes and went back to her notes. Should have kept his mouth shut.

Beyond her he saw Fiction A-E. He rushed over, skimming the books. He put one in front of her.

'*Breakfast at Tiffany's.*'

Smiling, she took the book back to the shelf. At least she smiled, he thought. You're in there my lad.

She came back with a Penguin Classic.

'*Great Expectations.*'

He moved further down the shelves. When he came back, he stood before her, presenting the paperback and swaying his hips.

'*Lord of the Flies.*'

She looked down her nose at it. 'Pity it's not in hard covers.'

Not a woman to be messed with.

Back to Fiction A-E. The Jane Austen omnibus.

'*Persuasion?*'

She just flicked the pages.

'*Sense And Sensibility.*'

He should have seen that coming.

He frantically scanned the shelves.

'*The Name Of The Rose?*'

Jane Austen was still on the table.

'*Emma.*'

A name, good. He ran along the fiction shelves, desperate to fix a date.

Shy, he slid the book to her, cover down. She turned it over.

'*Saturday Night, Sunday Morning.*'

She pocketed her notes and left the other books behind her. As she headed for the exit a title caught her eye. She turned it, spine down on the shelf, threw a smile at him and walked away.

He smiled back, cool. The moment her back was turned he sprinted to the shelf.

'*On The Road.*'

He turned to the entrance. The revolving door was still spinning.

Man's Best Friend

—LORNA MCCOOK

I sat in the doctors surgery waiting room. The pale blue walls seem to be getting closer the longer I wait. My left foot shakes a little as it does sometimes when I'm nervous.

I hate seeing my GP. I feel such a failure. Still on anti depressants two years after my wife died. Other men seem to move on a lot quicker and get married even. Stan at work married his second wife six months after his wife Mary died. My Gracie isn't so easy to replace. She was the love of my life. When she looked at me, I felt ten feet tall. When she hugged me, I could feel her giving me strength. She made me feel superhuman and I miss her terribly.

Bored, I started reading the various posters and notices on the walls.

One in particular, caught my attention. It read 'Get fit, Get a dog'. I had considered getting a rescue dog on and off for a few years now, but my grief has been all consuming. This felt like a lightbulb moment. I read somewhere that dogs can be therapeutic and can help these who are ill or disabled. I definitely could do with some healing. Battersea Dog's Home it is then.

Sheba seemed to have chosen me as her own. No one quite knows what breed or make she is, but many have offered theories. Among them collie, bulldog and even chihuahua. Sheba is beautiful to me with a very calm temperament. The first time she saw me she walked up to me and sat quietly, looking into my face. The other dogs would get excited or totally ignore me but she seemed quietly confident that she was the one. We felt connected straight away. Whenever I became overcome with grief, she would console me by patting my leg gently with a paw and then resting her chin on my lap looking up at me sympathetically. Our walks together were fun and gradually became longer with each passing week. My clothes gradually became loose and my hours of thinking about Gracie diminished. Sheba didn't mind other dogs as long as I didn't pat them or show them too much interest. I gradually became familiar with the local dog lovers and my social life became busier than ever. Sheba was part of this of course and rarely left my side.

We met Ruth and her German shepherd Milo on one of our walks. They were new to the area so the least I could do was offer to show them around the local sites and places of interest. Strangely, Sheba didn't mind me paying attention to Milo or his mum Ruth. The dogs hit it off straight away and played happily together. Six months later Ruth is my best friend and wife with our dogs coming a close second.

That Killer, Anxiety
—ARIS TSONTZOS

Alarm, alarm, alarm, alarm, alarm. Eyes open. Look at clock. Time to wake but want sleep still. Want not awake. Five more minutes, maybe. Not ready yet to face big mean day. Can manage five more minutes and still make work on time. Okay—that is okay. I am okay.

Eyes open again. Again look at clock. Should have woken ago twenty minutes. Late now. Oh shit oh shit oh shit. Got to rush. Got to get up, breakfast, coffee, wash, dress, prepare lunch, pack bag, leave house, walk to squash on train, enter office, work hard, make targets, do presentation, win client, make boss happy, come home, cook dinner, wash up, clean house, go to bed. Need to plan perfectly, need to complete perfect plan. Need be perfect.

Again open eyes. Look at clock again. Now late thirty minutes. Shit—now really late. Plan ruined. Maybe miss breakfast? No, will be hungry and work not good. Miss coffee? No, will be tired and grumpy. Need be productive. Need be nice, charming, make friends. Miss wash? No—will smell and make bad impression. Need make good impression, win client, win day. Lunch. Lunch can go. Will buy lunch instead, scrimp and save. Maybe small dinner. Will be okay. Just need to win day. Still have 45 minutes for leave house. Can still win.

Okay now. Feet, floor, kitchen. Toast in toaster. Set to three? Three is optimal brown, I think. But maybe today more crunchy is better? Four? No, four is too brown. Maybe. Too much crunch. Three point five. Three point five is perfect.

Lever down, wait wait wait. Going to be late. 40 minutes. Will make coffee. Pull cafetière from shelf. Boil water (not too much water in kettle so not waste energy), measure two level scoops coffee, pour in boiled water and stir with spoon for thirty seconds. Ten stirs. Must leave four minutes thirty seconds. Toast pops. Get butter, get jam. Must spread butter evenly—not too much will get fat. Now jam. Not too much jam for overpower butter. Forgot coffee! Shit. Maybe ruined. Get mug, press coffee, pour. Enjoy. Shove toast in mouth, but enjoy. Now wash.

Jump in shower. Pour just enough shampoo so not waste. Now shower gel—just right amount. Scrub, scrub, scrub. Am clean? Maybe scrub more. Maybe scrub too much damage skin. Oh shit. Check clock: 25 minutes. Need hurry.

Teeth. Brush. Two minutes. Brush brush brush. Spit. Is blood? Oh no. Brush too hard? Should stop, but not two minutes. What do? Look clock. 15 minutes. Shit—need to go.

Bedroom. Wardrobe. Trousers, on. Socks, on. Shirt, little creased, bad ironing, will new client see? Blazer. Will wear blazer.

Shoes. Laptop into bag, plus need charger. Where is charger? No time. Clock says 5 minutes. Look for charger. Is there in plug! Zip into bag. Oh shit—late! Run!

Outside, slam door. Need run fast for train. Cross road. Red car zoom.

The bear that ruined the wedding / Like the very gods in my sight

—HAN SMITH

What I had brought was an album of photographs, most of rivers and some of lakes. But the gesture was eclipsed, along with its motives, by the arrival of the bear.

The box was brought in and the guests were gathered. The mother of the bride introduced an old friend. The friend, as she explained herself, had been married to a man who had worked at a zoo. He had devoted his years to the animals as if they were his brothers, or his children, said the wife.

The bear had died of a lung infection, and the old friend's husband had been distraught. For the first time in decades he was completely unable to work. The idea had come to her then, said the wife. In those days these matters had been easier to arrange. Soon enough the bear was brought home as a skin to cover the tiles in the hallway. It was the thought of his feet on familiar fur that had got her husband back out in the world.

The wife glanced from her notes to beam at the guests.

Now her husband was ill in a new way, and had recently been moved to a place where care was always ensured. The old friend tapped her stick and reported that she was weakening and ageing too, that soon she would be moving to join her husband. The facility had already been asked about the bear but clearly they were not keen. And now the wedding, for the daughter of such a loyal, long-known friend.

As the cardboard box was opened and the contents spread out to be touched, I saw only the father of the bride hold back. The gift he had announced just minutes before was a cabinet organ that needed restoring. He stood with the single, still dam-aged pipe he had offered proudly as demonstration.

I watched him watch the fingers that dared to caress the head and fangs. I contemplated briefly the irrelevance we shared and how far I'd travelled to come. For a glance at the photographs it might have been worth it. The groom embraced the bride on the emptied bear no longer a brother, and I turned from the woman I had loved in a river, late in spring, too long ago.

Knife
—TOM O'BRIEN

I stepped forward so his knife dug into my gut. The pain was stunning. High and white as skin broke and flesh tore. Then dark and howling red as the blade lodged inside me, ripping a pathway through my organs.

Confusion replaced cockiness on his face. I was the victim. He was the thief. Victims weren't meant to impale themselves on the threat knife. Not meant to grab their assailant and lock them together.

'I needed this,' I said, close as a kiss. Hugging him, I knotted my fingers behind his back, sealing the stab between us. His aftershave stung my nose as I felt my stubble scratch his skin.

I tilted my head back and called out loud enough for anyone to hear. It was a noise, not a word, but it broadcast fear and distress on the quiet city side street that no one could ignore.

The distress was real. My head lightened as I held him close. He swore and staggered and tried to untangle himself but we were slickly knotted. There must be so much blood. My instinct was to put my hand to it but I couldn't let him go.

Bile rose. I leaned my head forward onto the shoulder of this man who had selected me from the flock of commuters headed home. Once separated from the safety of the group he had strode past me, then turned, blocking my path, pointing a weapon. For what? Money, my wedding ring, credit cards, phone, my ready meals for one?

I never found out.

Whatever he had planned, this is what he had.

I had a flutter of panic that I could die. I clung tighter as

I heard shouts on the street. My call had been heard. Footsteps, running. Voices. Some hesitant, others forceful, all closing, rising. Someone on the phone to the police. I could hear but not see. Under the streetlight my bloodied dance partner filled my vision. His squirming told me they were close. My fingers tightened behind his back as my legs weakened.

'Thank you,' I said, as we were untangled. He had taken control from me. It had been the only thing holding me together. I stole it back from the tip of his blade.

On the cold ground I looked down to see that my hand had finally found the blood. It pooled and sucked around the knife but all I could see, as my eyes closed, was my wedding ring. If I woke my guilt might be bearable. She had been taken, not me. I would not ask why anymore. On a quiet street on an ordinary night, a stranger with a short steel knife had shown me there was no why.

Kookaburra Sweet *(an excerpt)*
—IRENOSEN OKOJIE

At the flat, she fell asleep in the bedroom. When she woke up, her body felt supple, soft, bendy, unfamiliar. She spotted a dark stain on the blue bed sheet. She looked at it with suspicion, rubbed the spot. Her fingers were black, liquorice coloured, stretchy. Her heart rate tripled. She leapt off the bed somewhat unsteadily. Rushed to the mauve coloured bathroom, skin care products lined the edges of the tub, crowded the sink. She accidentally knocked over a bottle of Palmers Cocoa Butter Crème in her haste. Her toothbrush went flying. She switched on the light. The 60 watt bulb stuttered in anticipation as she rushed to the mirror, light flickering sporadically as though arguing with itself. Chest heaving, she starred at her reflection, her breath pale magician's smoke. Sure enough she was not herself. Or, she was herself but something different. Something skewed and accidental, something tainted with the margin particles of an incense smelling man who could mimic the curves of a sidewinder. Her bathroom had become a circus balancing on two hinges, rocking unsteadily in the ether. She took tentative steps closer to the mirror. Sure enough she had transformed into liquorice; a black, sweet liquorice woman, a liquorice sweet black woman; bendy, stretchy, adaptable in harsh conditions, resplendent and irrepressible. Reconfigured heart oozing liquid midnight, necessary external jaggedness flung out like day traps, moist turning tongue set anti-clockwise to catch soft light, soft memory, soft landing. She turned the taps on for the sound of the sea to fill the sink and tub. All that came through was bursting, rushing water. She placed her hand under the cold tap, the weight of water bending her fingers slightly. She used her right hand to adjust them back, then raised both hands to water her head with night dew. She turned the cold tap off. The blast of hot water meant the pipes started whistling. Slowly, then speedily, panicked by the possibilities of changes tumbling through their lengthy, corroded bodies. She pressed her fingers into her head, feeling her way around for a crack. Steam misted the mirror. She didn't want to melt. Melting meant not existing. She turned the hot water tap off, waiting for the whistling to stop. She started screaming.

The fading sounds of the chugging pipes mutated into an alarm ringing in her head. Anxiety spread from the very heart of her, a burning sensation in her new body. Sydney had been a disaster. She was broken by it. Almost. She stepped back away from the mirror, trying to weigh the ache within, the losses she'd left on Sydney harbour turning to twisted currencies glowing in the dark, the octopus shaped critter that had tried to gain entry into her suitcase to find a corner to possess. She pressed her mouth against that corner to breathe, to steady herself; loss of confidence, loss of income, loss of heart, loss of lover. The ache inside her grew into a kite shaped slipstream spotted with silver. She started to cry, heaving sobs threatening to become accomplices in the cramped bathroom. She needed to fill the ache, to do something. It was open house week after all. She grabbed a black bin bag from the top of the cabinet.

Around 1AM she wandered the streets, bin bag in tow. Squishy sounds of her new limbs kept her company. She walked to the sprawling Horniman Museum gardens, found nothing to catch except the reflection of her old self in the café's glass doors and windows. That Kara had gone to Australia chasing a story; a dreadlocked molasses hued man who believed his lost mother appeared to him during volcano eruptions, who took tender photographs that captured her silhouette exiting those eruptions. Kara had wanted to write his story but the man gave her heart to a volcano for his mother to eat. On the steep London Road, she entered the white houses through windows left open. She gathered from the inhabitants things most people would never take during open house; the post office clerk's fear of failure, the sweet shop assistant's paranoia he'd die before doing half the items on his bucket list, the glint from the blade the kebab shop owner used to carve scenes for three stillborn babies trapped in a revolving winter, the deli owner's conversations to the gremlin he'd transplanted into his chest, that kept trying to break ceilings with a long, slimy tentacle. She wandered through houses while people slept, humming the tune Kizzy sang at the airport, leaving a trail of deep, warm sweetness, stuffing her bag until it was fit to burst. When she arrived back home, the bin liner split on her bed, on the crumpled tulip patterned duvet. The things she'd caught had charred wings and were flapping towards possible exits frenetically. White airbags sprung from the corners of her bed, shrieking incessantly before the air left them twisted into mean, sunken expressions. And the sharp pain exploding in Kara's chest before liquefying was unbearable.

After discovering that a last self collision resulted in change you couldn't foresee, Kara limped out onto the Dartmouth road the next morning, having caught her left foot in a trap she'd flung from herself. She clutched her plane ticket to Sydney, a sacrificial woman in the heat hollering Kizzy's song about becoming what you eat. It was bright out. The day was alcoholic. As she sang, her body began to separate. Her head went first, tossed into the blind spot of a sputtering drunk holding a Guiness can like a lover. Her head shrank rapidly. Her legs came off, tumbling backwards into an argument between the off license owner and a woman holding a leash without a dog she claimed she'd lost at Heathrow airport. Kara's golden eyes uprooted into the traffic, speedily rolling between lanes, between tires, frantically blinking away images of a life that were discarded receipts for

gutted angels with streaks of black tears on their faces, reduced
to husks on the bent skyline. Her arms were dark boomerangs
confused by an unplanned separation, the dizziness of slow
traffic in the sky, attempting to embrace satellite dishes, anten-
nas, and items that found their way to rooftops while the road
swelled with resignation of a split, of a break somewhere that
saw small creatures from accidents with Kara's last heartbeats
mutating in their chests as they scurried onto the pavements on
either side, leaving patches of unleaded fuel and kaleidoscopic
red in their attempts to talk. Residents from cafes and the bou-
tique, village like stores and eateries including The Hill Lounge
and Kitchen and Bird In Hand spilled out onto the street watching. Two assistants from Sugar Mountain sweet shop abandoned
its light, tantalising atmosphere of deep booths, board games
and seductive retro sweets in large jars. They rushed out carrying a jar each to catch bits of Kara's body. People from Forest
Hill Pools filed out barefoot onto the pavement still in their cos-
tumes, dripping translucent daydreams doubling as swimming
strokes beneath the sun. The locals were chess pieces held
still by a human combustion on a glimmering day. Kara's thighs
spun. One slid down a lamppost, leaving a dark, honey like trail
before becoming stuck at the bottom. The other slid across the
window display of Il Mirto's Italian deli and Ice Cream store. Her
head now reduced to pulp was being lapped up by the drunk on
all fours in abandon. His tongue darting greedily, the Guiness
can forgotten, squashed under his knee, pennies spilling from
his pocket like a marauding coppery fountain. Kara's mouth was
sylph like, chased by an aboriginal cowboy's hat into the distance
before it melted onto the rim in the shape of an atom bursting,
an accidental decoration. Her scattered teeth were white jewels
for the afternoon. A stuntman man in a diving costume caught
her vagina, sucking on it like the nectar of a goddess. Her hands
were clasped together, prayer like while bits of clouds morphed

into the shapes of temporary pale clothing for the inhabitants of Forest Hill to wear as the uniform of witnesses. After their naïve prayer, her hands eventually melted on the wheel of a dented blue Ford Cortina that would run out of fuel later. And all that was left was the morning to come. All that was left was her torso on the edge; black, gleaming, edible, sweet. Liquorice sweet. Full of warped, rhapsodic song in the traffic.

—*CONTINUED ON SPREADTHEWORD.ORG.UK*

Herd and Splinter
—AARON COX

Up until then, I hadn't realised I'd been rehearsing for this moment all my life. Imagining quietly what I might do. In my mind. Not knowing when it might occur. It's night. Late enough to be in bed, not eating. The steak is divine. Jehan and I, we're sitting outside under an awning. There's commotion somewhere behind me. Revellers. I pay little attention. Then I suddenly notice that the light over there is the same off yellow as the sponge I use to clean my bathroom. I can't see so well. Globs of red rain fall on my face and hands. It's strange, I can't remember the name of the play we'd been talking about, Jehan and I. From across the table, words shriek from her eyes. Quick. Move. Runn! My cutlery is glued to my hands. I can't see too well. We herd. All of us. We herd and splinter. A stampeded of animals. Down the street. Down dark alleys. My shoes are back at the table. I've never liked running barefoot. Too much glass. But I can't stop. I must follow the strangers. Jehan, I call. Jehan! I've lost her. So much glass, slowing me down. I see a policeman. A lone policeman standing against the herd. Plucking people out of the crowd. He catches me as I pass. What have I done? I say. What have I done? You can put those down now, he says and takes the knife and the fork from my blood-soaked hands. I need you to hide down there. Can you manage that? I look at the faces in the cavernous basement. No Jehan. Then I look back to where I came from and face the jaws of terror, with their sharp, masticating blades. Is the colour of love really the colour of blood? I puke. The policeman grips my wrist like I'm a child. Can you manage? he says dragging me towards the stairs. When he lets go, he takes blood

94

S | LEWISHAM

from my skin. He's going to die standing there. As I fall down the stairs, shots ring out. A shot. A shot. A shot. A shot. For a moment I am caught in a web of screams before I collapse into the belly of silence.

Crying Cobalt Blue
—YOVANKA PAQUETE PERDIGAO

As soon as I came home, I threw my school uniform on the floor of the bathroom. It was sticky with fear and sweat. I got under the shower, desperately wanting the water to wash away the earlier memories of that day. I looked at my uniform sprawled on the floor. Specks of blood had bloomed on the cobalt blue dress. I imagined the school director, Madame Padovani's face melting at the sight of the now plum flowers on her beloved school's uniform. The dress was simple and modest, nothing exceptional besides the vibrant blue inspired by the school's mascots. Cocky birds whose imperious blue feathers and viridescent mane were the school's signature of French academic excellence, paraded through school halls unbothered by its pupils. It was in fact one of the peacocks, sitting majestically by the school fountain, that had warned me of the terrible things to come. My father had been late for pick-up so I was loitering around the fountain when I heard the peacock's cries. A long mournful sound that stopped time, I could no longer hear the other children playing, the teachers pressing to go home or the busy parents. I turned to look at the animal meeting his purple eyes. They were like a never ending well of tears, I edged closer to the bird and heard a faint whistling sound. I immediately crouched to the ground recognizing the commotion that was about to follow. Eyes began to water, noises shrivelled, and within seconds there was crying and screaming. Tear bombs were raining. 'The rebels are coming', someone shouted sending everyone in a panic frenzy. School children ran scattered in all directions. Teachers ran after them attempting to impose order but they were also afraid.

Parents called out desperately after their children, trying to fight their panic. Suddenly the sound of gunshot reverberated through the school. It danced around for a few minutes, diving in each nook and cranny before finally choosing its target. The bird's eyes went backwards as he fell into the school fountain. I just stood over the water watching it turn crimson. I heard my father's voice calling me. I turned and saw him fighting through the smoke and waved at him. He walked as if we were on the beach and not in the middle of avoiding tear gas. He tried to sound calm, but his voice was shaky when he said: 'Don't run.' I looked at him and simply said, 'There is nowhere to run.' We stood together looking at the bird, now completely submerged by water, as chaos surrounded us. My father, always superstitious, found time to dig through his pocket for change and tossed a coin. I let out a long sigh. Unlike the others around us, we knew what this all meant and this was just the beginning. Beyond the smell of tear gas, the sweat clinging to school uniforms, and the frantic cries was the beginning of war.

Daredevil
—SIMON HIGGS

A tall, bald, overweight guy in glasses sits at the end of the dimly lit bar with his back to me. He has an affected camp lilt, a voice that carries, and he's wielding it, arguing with a tattooed barman over the difference between a Whisky Mac, which he ordered, and a Scotch & American, which he's been served.

I've heard this exchange before and it sends me tumbling back into a student house I shared—three girls and two boys, a ménage-a-cinq, bed-hopping through the first year in Smalltown, England. Katy, Kerry, Annabelle, Sebastian and Me.

I screwed Katy first, and Sebastian last, at last, and even then only due to a particularly drunken threesome, when Kerry had double dared us. No one loved anyone, it was all about sex. Except Annabelle who loved herself, and me, belatedly, waking to an overarching ache for Sebastian.

These days being gay is relatively easy, love dares to speak its name, but then, not even at my most devilish I would not have dared the word 'love'. We could justify the fucking: I was 'experimenting' and Sebastian, well Sebastian would hit me—black eyes and bruised ribs became my accessories. It was his way of trying to cope, not with the love of cock, that was palatable, but his need at night to sleep in the arms of another man.

I knew, of course, that this overweight bald guy at the bar with his Scotch & American was, somehow, Sebastian. His laugh gave him away—all the preening, pouting and camped-up language was undone by a laugh that had haunted me for twenty years. I listened to him speak in this odd 'new' voice, wondering how long he'd been using it. I was waiting, I realised in my stupidity, for him to say, 'I was in love with this guy once, long ago, I wish I had been able to tell him.'

Annabelle was modelling back then, Sebastian accompanied her to a shoot and the agency snapped him up; the pair of them were sent to Spain for the summer on assignment.

He didn't say goodbye, he hated hospitals and he really hadn't meant to put me into one: he'd come sobbing one night, having a hard time coming out to his parents and, helpfully, I pointed out 'if they hadn't wanted a gay son then they wouldn't have named you Sebastian, they'd have gone for Derek, or something a little straighter.' So I provoked him, but then I'd known when he came in sobbing that I was going to get his fist.

They settled in Barcelona and Annabelle gave birth to a girl, after that I cut myself off from them all.

I got up to leave, straightening knees sent chair legs scraping across the wooden floor and, although I did not look up, momentarily I was visible. Upon exit I heard him call my name, I'm not sure now which voice he used, and I didn't dare turn back.

Some Family Recipes are not Written Down
—ANITA GOVEAS

Nana said 'I'll be judged on your daal', as they squeezed into her tiny kitchen. 'Almost ten years old! You're starting late, we'll see what we can do.'

Dada and Mumma had gone to the market, and Nana had turned off Scooby-Doo. They were surrounded by spice bottles, dull grey pans hanging from the ceiling. Felcy kept bumping into ladles on the hanging-rack and the spiky-edged aloe vera on the windowsill. Papa didn't cook, he'd give himself concussion. Clusters of leaves from the badam tree were poking through the window, Papa showed her the baby almonds yesterday.

The temperature outside was 29 degrees, a heat only experienced in Luton when she'd accidentally walked into a sauna. Mumbai was different. Her chapaals kept falling off, she couldn't squeeze her toes together properly. Her chin-length hair, 'so short you look like a boy,' had puffed up like a damp mushroom. Her green cotton t-shirt was sticking to her, Miss Piggy's face crumpling up in disgust. But the onions were sizzling, Nana was pulling out jars of seeds Felcy had never seen before and she was mesmerised by the gas-stove. Mumma let her put trays of fish-fingers in the oven, but not take them out. This was the closest she'd been to a flame since the 'making cheese in a milk-bottle' incident.

'Try this', and Nana put something that tasted of earth in her open mouth. 'Don't use anything if you don't know what it tastes like.'

As the sharp onion smell became sweet, Nana added red lentils. A black, shiny, penny-sized blob scuttled across the wall. 'You add the water. ' Nana handed her a jug and removed her chapaal. Felcy stretched up to tip the water in, the glugging mixing with the banging of the sandal on the tiled wall.

'Ants, they're extra protein,' Nana said, leaning on Felcy's shoulder to replace the sandal. 'Cockroaches don't taste good if they fall in.'

As the lentils turned yellow, smelling savory and sounding cheerful, Nana started dry-frying the cumin seeds for the garnish.

'Why's your mother keeping you out of the kitchen? Da'Souza women are natural cooks.' Mumma hadn't told about the cheese experiment then. Felcy held the mustard seeds. As she trickled them into the pan, she watched them pop to see if they had legs.

When Mumma caught her picking ants off their garden-wall in Luton, when she was supposed to be packing her school-bag, Felcy explained. 'There's no mustard seeds. Nana said I can't use these in the daal till I know what they taste like.' She offered a wriggling insect squeezed between two fingers. 'Want one? Protein's important.'

Seer, Unseen
—VICKY RICHARDS

'There is a troll living under Tower Bridge!' I shout. My voice may be rough and coarse, but it still rings loud. Today could be the day.

'I've seen it,' I continue, as the passers-by skirt around me. 'Don't you see it now? That huge black body climbing the nearby tower?'

People come and go like flies beneath the outlines of the bridge. An ice cream van trills its merry tune. A woman clutches her beady blonde son against her side like a talisman. She looks wounded just to see me.

'Can you really not see it?' I ask the blankness in her eyes.

I dreamed about it at first, like some dark fiction. Tossing and turning in the sweaty cocoon of my sleeping bag, I saw its grasping touch on the one London landmark I still liked, and I knew I had to go and look.

The dank summer air brushed my face like wildfire as I shuffled down the South Bank. Empty streets and empty smiles were all I encountered; the trees of the embankment danced in the darkness overhead. I remember liking this invincible twilight.

At the bridge, I waited for it and it came. Rising from the water in its wet, formidable shape. I call it a troll, but it is something from before clay, before man. It was like seeing liquid oil settle into the stocky, paralysing shape of a human. I could almost understand it.

I am still upright, crossing and re-crossing the paths of tourists with my message. Today could be the day. I am like a prophet for this beast, ready to smear the stain of its existence onto people. My arsenal of cardboard posters say the same thing in different thicknesses of heavy marker pen:

'There is a troll living under Tower Bridge. Why can't you see it?'

The crowd looks right through me like a shadow. Sometimes I think that's why it called me. I wonder increasingly if we are one and the same—both invisible creatures in this world. I wonder what it would be like to ease myself into the river, let my body unfurl itself into reams of inky blackness, let myself be carried away on the currents to rebuild into some primeval form.

All these people, and yet not one of them can let themselves imagine its existence. Not one of them can think past the exterior of their own thick skulls.

The woman and her son have gone, but a man is watching me now. He is all shine—from his haircut to his shoes—with even a slick, glossy voice to match. His eyes hold the small sparkle of interest I have so often tried to create. Today could be the day.

He throws his cigarette butt at my feet. I watch as the used fire burns out and its small light is finally extinguished.

Washed Up
—LUCINDA OFFER

Few people ventured down the slippery steps to stumble along the exposed strip of muddy rocks and centuries of detritus next to the murky Thames.

Tonight, low tide coincided with an argument between her mum and stepdad, so she left with Henry, her spaniel. He bounded ahead of her, fanned tail wagging. She scanned the uneven stones and rubble for any fresh treasures deposited by the receding water. Looking across the wide, brown expanse of river, she could see lights on the skyscrapers of Canary Wharf, a dense cluster of global banking behemoths.

She stopped and examined some fragments of pottery and dark brown bones of long-dead animals, far too old to interest Henry. He was investigating what appeared to be a dead fish, to the consternation of several gulls which squawked indignantly. The light was starting to fade and she almost tripped on a rusting microwave which was slowly filling with mud and stones. A Thames Clipper roared past in the middle of the river and its wake sent strong waves to the shore, disturbing the gulls. Henry gave up on the fish and ran along the edge of the water. Suddenly he began to bark at an object on top of one of the wooden piles which were all that remained of the old docks.

'What is it, boy?' she asked, walking over to join him. He continued the barking frenzy so she switched her smartphone flashlight on and followed the direction of his gaze. The object of his excitement looked like a plastic crate, left atop a pile by the outgoing tide and surrounded by swirling water. As the sound of the waves died down, she could hear a baby crying. She looked around but then realised with a jolt of horror that it was coming from the box in the water. She picked up a plank of driftwood and tried to test the depth of the water but the current almost ripped it from her hands.

Shaking, she dialled 999 and explained the situation to the calm operator. He told her to wait there for the RNLI and under no circumstances to enter the water. The crying seemed to be getting quieter and she was terrified that the baby was weakening. Tears fell as images filled her head of who might have dumped a baby in the river. A scared teenage mother? A frustrated, angry father?

She saw a bright light coming closer across the water.

'Over here!' she shouted, while Henry barked.

A man leant out of the inflatable lifeboat and grabbed the box. She saw him examine the contents and then speak to a colleague, his shoulders shaking.

'I'm so sorry, I didn't find it in time,' she cried.

One of the men turned to her and called. 'It's alright love, no need to cry, it's only a doll. The water must've short circuited it.'

Alice
—LYNNE COUZINS

Alice is a loner, she doesn't make friends. She has terrible nightmares, damp dark places with scratching noises and a touch on her skin that wakes her with a shudder. She says she has had them all her life, beginning in a childhood that she can't remember. There is something about Alice, some otherworldly quality that sets her apart from the other residents in the home. Maybe it comes from living a lifetime in her own magical version of reality.

Alice is a magpie. At the end of every day she emerges from her room long enough to search the dayroom for treasures. Lengths of thread and ribbon pulled from clothing by grasping, agitated fingers, escaping beads and fallen buttons are all gathered into her tin. Even soft feathers from the budgie cage and shed hairs from the cat, her only friend who is as aloof as she, are carefully collected.

Her tin is full now. Alice goes out late one afternoon on her mobility scooter, her crutches in their holders behind her seat. When she gets to the walled fairy garden in the park she dismounts and retrieves her crutches, slipping her tin into her pocket. She climbs determinedly up the narrow path to the middle of the garden. There she hangs all the bright threads and ribbons over branches and stems. She places buttons and beads into flowers, carefully weighing down the feathers and hair. Lengths of lace flutter in tall ornamental grasses. Her favourite big glass bead she lays gently in the soft petals of a red rose, her favourite flower. Then she picks her way back to her scooter and charges for the main gate. The keeper is there with his keys, waiting. 'No rush' he calls but Alice is enjoying the unaccustomed burst of speed.

The next morning Alice is out early and races back to the park. She doesn't know what she is expecting, but anticipation is riding on her shoulder. The main gates are open for dog walkers but she knows the walled garden won't be unlocked until the keepers start work. She heads there anyway and even from a distance she can see a small patch of bright colours against the black gate. Alice approaches and there, hanging from a black iron scroll, is a perfectly formed miniature dreamcatcher. Alice lays it in her hand and inspects it. She can see all her treasures woven in, even plaited cat hairs, radiating out from the glass bead at the centre. Only the tiniest, most nimble fingers could have created such beautiful perfection and a dreamcatcher, as if someone sees her sleep.

Alice always wakes with a smile now as she opens her eyes to see her enchanted gift twirling in the morning light. She doesn't know if it is a fairy charm that has made the difference or just the magic that comes from one small act of kindness.

A New and Better World
—OKSANA WENGER

Crashing waves made Sami plummet, down into the groaning sea. Soon the dappled shadows darkened and everything was in slow-motion. He glided past a succession of arches resting on cylindrical pillars then grabbed onto some seaweed to stop himself from sliding down a mossy staircase to where the cavernous depths lay.

Sami knew he mustn't get distracted; he had to free himself from the embrace of the slimy tentacles. He kicked and pushed himself away. He wished he'd taken his uncle's advice and got fitter for the journey. Instead, while at the market stall, he'd preferred to study his English phrasebook. At quiet times he'd wander over to the stall opposite and share his dreams with the beautiful and sympathetic Sulaf.

But then the bombing had begun and people dispersed to the harsher but safer rural areas. Sulaf was one of these and so was Sami's mother. Sami and his uncle made their way to the harbour with their savings, in the hope of escaping the barbarity. For Sami any city would do. He'd work in a restaurant, clean, wash up, anything. Then one day he'd be reunited with Sulaf and his family.

Not long into the journey he'd been overwhelmed by hunger. He fantasised about the possibility of catching fish. It was then that the dinghy was hurtled against the rocks as if by the hand of a giant. Desperately clinging to the side, Sami called out his uncle's name, hopelessly. He'd thought about his stomach while his heart was being wrenched from him.

Once the dinghy landed, the crying stopped and the screaming began. It was more like a wailing of a hundred souls as they took their last gasp. Earlier, when his uncle had questioned the safety of the vessel, the captain had smirked 'no problem'. He'd held out his hand for payment as he ushered the swarm of people on board. They set sail in the calmness. Silently they were all squashed together. His uncle held his hand, his eyes closed as if praying. The sea was as placid as a bowl of soup and everyone began smiling or humming, glad to be heading to a new and better world.

Without warning the storm arrived, a full-blown gale, merciless and indiscriminate. Sami had tied his belt to the dinghy as instructed, but it was no use; the winds catapulted the dinghy like a dragon regurgitating its breakfast. He managed to stay attached for an age but then something hit him on the head and all became iciness and struggle.

If only he could reach the top to breath. He knew he didn't have long. But the depths called out to him so sweetly. It would be so easy to succumb to this serenity, away from the unfairness and the strife.

Abruptly he felt a harshness at his underarms, yanking him upwards. The new and better world had slipped away from him. He'd have to make it on dry land now. He might just have a chance.

A Bench, a Scar
—SOPHIE RONALD

Cabs are scuttling past, shining black beetles honking their horns as I weave across the road. I breathe out and duck down Harewood Place. There are no birds singing in the trees, no parakeets in this part of town, I can't smell cherry blossom; just this morning's rain and last night's beer dregs in cans by the bin. I was once told that our grief makes us a colony; others don't want to come close for fear of catching it, and we the affected are all together. I don't feel that. I feel alone with mine. I don't share it with the colony; I share it with this park. Your bench is newly wood-stained; we did it for what would have been your birthday. We ate sandwiches and drank Champagne out of plastic cups like so many other Londoners that weekend, punctuating parks around the city with chatter, cheers and pigeon shoo-ing.

'Do you mind if I sit here?' I ask some tourists. They say they don't but they are looking at me like I'm mad and scan the park looking at all of the benches without occupants. Your plaque is cold under my hand and I touch it like I would a font at the church entrance—partly out of habit, partly out of respect and mainly out of some misguided searching will for it to be true that you are still here, in some sense, just behind the hub-ub of Oxford Street still with me.

The last day that I saw you we sat in this park, we ate icecreams, I tugged at the yellowing grass beneath me and I took photos of you on an old Kodak, but the film never came out. I must have unloaded it in sunlight or something. I wasn't thinking straight much in those months afterwards. You were on your lunch break from your work placement. A twenty year old in a suit.

It was an unseasonably hot day and our Celtic roots betrayed as we turned rose in the light. I can't remember what we spoke about, not a lot I expect.

After our Cornettos I went over to Shepherds Bush to a house party. I got warm fuzzy drunk, threw up in a Roses tin and fell asleep under some coats with the night time city air breathing in from a cracked window, fried chicken was heavy in the air, I could hear the foxes outside. It felt like we were invincible that spring.

Flat
—JOANNE GALE

Golden, evening light started filling our carriage and despite the train still running six minutes behind, most people had given up complaining. We crawled past a packed pub beer garden; bustling with people who could find seats and afford London pints. My colleague sighed. We'd met early this morning, bright and coffee pumped, but today had been unusually hot and physically challenging. Our muscles ached—chatting was now a welcome, painless activity.

We'd discussed the agency and he'd explained how he'd recently bought new veneers—had cut down to seventy fags a week. I'd made an estimated total cost—we were earning the same hourly rate; watching internet videos was the only addiction I could afford. The right sole of my shoe had broken. The agency hadn't called about work for tomorrow and my rent was still due next week.

The train passed several large concrete structures, nestled close to the tracks. An impressive metal crane lingered behind. 'Where'd you live?' my colleague snorted. 'North. Zone 5,' I smiled weakly. His neck clicked. 'We'd thought about that— far for work. They gave us a three bed, Zone 2 when we first moved—wouldn't consider further out now.' His veneers pushed out his top lip significantly. 'My Wife's thinking we should buy another flat; more investment you know. You married?' he flashed the veneers. I shook my head—my smile fell away. He looked younger in the evening light. I'd rather stay silent then say aloud that I have no property or family at my age.

A hiss click—I noticed a group of four smartly dressed people sat across from us. One was sipping a chain store hot drink, the others canned G&Ts. I made an estimated total cost of the drinks—more than today's hourly wage; costing like this was an awful habit, but I couldn't afford to stop.

The train pulled into the station. We shared a short goodbye and my leg cramped a little as I minded the gap and joined the crowds heading for the underground. The agency still hadn't called.

I paused next to other waiting commuters. Backlit by the sunset I saw a group of angular, modern high rises, complimented by tiny balconies and a sign—Luxury flats. Sold. We started descending the stairs for the tunnels. I'd phoned another agency last week—asked if I could set my own hourly minimum wage. The employee laughed, 'If you want to struggle, sure.' I touched my card against a reader and made an estimated total cost for today's travel—roughly two hours of today's hourly wage. I boarded the tube.

Above ground, close to the station, the evening light still filled a pub beer garden. Pounds poured into London pints for those who could afford seats.

Over an hour later I perched on the edge of my bed and started eating supper. One day I hoped to be able to afford a table.

Rose and Crown
—ALEX WHEATLE

Kingston Square, sometime in the Victorian age.
'Thomas Crown! You'd better not be in bed. Where are you?
A gentleman has just arrived and his horses need stabling.'

Standing outside her Seven Kings and Ham Inn, the horses
shifted uneasily causing the mud to splash Rose's dress. 'Oh,
bloody hell!' Rose swore. 'I just washed this. Thomas Crown!
Get down here!'

Rose accepted the gentleman's luggage and beckoned him
inside. 'What name will it be, sir?'

'Charles, Charles Dickens.'

'And what do you do, Mr Charles, sir.'

'Oh, I dabble in a bit of writing.'

'Writing? I don't think we've ever had a man of letters before.
Welcome to my humble abode, Mr Charles, sir. How long will you
be staying?

'Just the one night, maybe two.'

'*Thomas!* Sorry, Mr Charles, sir. My husband's a bit hard of
hearing sometimes. *Thomas!*'

She led him through the front door and into a small reception room that had a counter on the left hand side for serving
ales and food. The kitchen was through another doorway. Thick
beams lined the uneven ceiling. Barrels were stacked against
the far wall. A wood fire glowed in a corner. Waxing candles sat
on wonky tables that were circled by three-legged stools. The
windows were thick with grime.

'*Thomas!* I could do with another pair of hands!'

Climbing the naked, creaking staircase, Rose glanced over

her left shoulder. 'I'll give you the best room in the house, Mr Charles, sir. It overlooks the market square and you can see all the wares and entertainment on a Saturday morning.'

'That's most kind of you, madam. How shall I address you?'

'That's lovely of you to ask, Mr Dickens, sir. Call me Rose.'

Offering Mr Dickens a key, she marched along to the end of the hallway and entered her own bedroom. She found Thomas sprawled on the bed. Drool leaked from his mouth. 'Get up! Get up! We have a gentleman guest! He's a man of letters so at least he'll know how much we're going to charge him. His horses need stabling and his carriage needs cleaning.'

Thomas rolled on to his back. The daylight caused him to squint. 'Can't you do it, Rose? I'm a bit indisposed.'

'Indisposed! You're indisposed! I was up with the larks this morning making Mr Grimmthorpe's breakfast. He wanted an early start with a side of ham. I had to wash the linen, sweep out the rooms, scrub out the back, fetch the milk...'

Thomas covered his ears. Rose continued. '...get some eggs in, barter for a side of ham, wash the jars, wipe the tables...'

'Will you shut up, Rose! It's Friday. I have half day off on Friday's.'

'You had the evening off yesterday,' Rose countered. 'Don't you think I saw you creeping off in the middle of the night to the Sledge and Muck?'

'I work hard all week,' Thomas protested. 'Am I not entitled to a few jugs of ale and join in a sing-song?'

'Not if you're buying ale from someone else! Now get down stairs and stable those horses and clean Mr Charles' coach! You know I don't like touching horses. And if they poop on my side-path, you can clean it up!'

'Nag, nag, nag! That's all I get with you, Rose. I'll find more peace in Bridewell prison.'

'Then be my guest and find a room there! I don't know what

they'll make of you there. You're about as much use to me as a stocking made of wet mud!'

Thomas wiped his face, picked out the matter from his eyes and slowly got up to his feet. Before he went downstairs, he offered Rose an evil glare.

'If you wanna be fed tonight, don't look at me like that, Thomas Crown,' Rose barked.

Sixteen hours later, Rose was preparing a dinner of goose, carrots and potatoes for Mr Dickens and three other guests. Thomas had cleaned the stables and groomed the horses but he was nowhere to be found.

'That bloody husband of mine!' Rose cursed. 'Always leaving me to cook on my own. I bet he's down the Sledge and Muck.'

A loud knock on the door interrupted her daydream of her husband suffering a most painful death. She opened the door to reveal a fat gentleman sporting a black bowler hat, a blue waist-coat, a skinny tie and carrying a cane.

'Mr Fullgrout,' Rose greeted. 'Shouldn't you be busy send-ing rogues, thieves and the ungodly to Bridewell prison? What brings you to my humble abode?'

'I'm afraid a complaint has been made, Mrs Crown.'

'A complaint?' Rose repeated. 'By the Lord, who?'

'By your husband, Mr Crown.'

'You jest with me, Mr Fullgrout.'

'Madam Crown! I would not waste time walking from my office through mud and sledge to arrive here in jest!'

'What is Thomas's complaint? The horses pooped on his breeches?'

Mr Fullgrout held the lapels of his jacket with his thumbs and fore-fingers. A window was opened above. Mr Dickens looked out of it.

'Of never-ending and most highly unpleasant nagging, Mrs Crown,' Mr Fullgrout finally replied. 'And I'm sure that you're aware of the punishment.'

Rose shook her head. 'I am aware that the law of this town is an *ass*! A gigantic *ass*! But Thomas would never complain about me.'

'I'm afraid he did, Madam Crown. Do you accept the customary punishment or would you rather spend a night or three in Bridewell prison? You may know that the rats, spiders and cockroaches that make their home there are not friendly.'

The next morning, Rose was led by Mr Fullgrout and two of his assistants to a nearby waterway where she was strapped into a ducking stool. Buyers and sellers of the market followed the procession. They jostled for a good vantage point. Some took to the rooftops. The rope was tied tight about Rose's wrists and waist. The dominantly male crowd whooped, laughed and hollered. The water was thick with flotsam, sewage and spoiled food that even the vagrants rejected. Rose closed her eyes and gritted her teeth. She could do nothing about the vile stench that attacked her nostrils. She promised herself not to scream.

The moment came.

She was suddenly dropped into the filthy pool. There she remained for two seconds before she was hoisted up again. The mob cheered and tossed their hats into the air. Rose tried her best to clear her eyes. She coughed, retched and spluttered.

Nightfall came but there was no sign of Thomas Crown. Rose sat in the kitchen. Her clothes drying on a wooden frame set around the fire. She whispered dark thoughts under her breath.

The back door opened and closed again. Rose looked up. She recognised her husband's footsteps. He entered the kitchen carrying a bag.

'You've got a nerve, Thomas Crown!' Rose roared. 'There's no bed for you tonight! You can sleep with the worms and beetles! Get out of here!'

'I'm sorry, Rose,' Thomas apologised. 'So sorry. I was stupid. I didn't think Mr Fullgrout would go through with it. I swear!'

'Did you watch?' Rose wanted to know. 'Tell me, Thomas

Crown. Did you watch the whole town laughing as I was dunked into that mucky pool? Did you? For the life of me I still can't get the smell out of my clothes.'

Thomas sat down at the kitchen table. 'Of course not, my dear. I was drunk when I made the complaint to Mr Fullgrout. I didn't think he'd go through with it.'

'You didn't think that he'd go through with it! Mr Fullgrout hates women! He committed his own mother to an asylum! He sent his own sister to Bridewell prison because she couldn't pay a debt.'

'I've…I've got something for you, Rose,' Thomas said. 'My way of saying sorry.'

Rose folded her arms and side-eyed her husband. 'What's that then? An iron chain and collar so I can drag you around Market Square?'

'No, my dear.' Thomas pulled out three fishes from his bag. 'Pikes! For tomorrow's lunch. I'm sure Mr Dickens and the other guests will enjoy this with bread.'

'And where did you get the money to buy those?' Rose wanted to know.

Thomas didn't reply. Instead, he gazed into the fire.

Rose smiled. 'You're right, Thomas. I'm sure our guests will love a fish lunch. I'll prepare it tonight.'

'Does that mean that I'm forgiven?' Thomas asked.

Rose thought about it. She remembered the taste of the soiled water filling her mouth and nostrils. She recalled the slime curling around her shoulders. 'You're forgiven,' she said. 'But if you complain about me again, you'll be sleeping with the rabbits and their droppings.'

The next day Thomas enjoyed a short nap following a fine lunch of pike, bread and carrots. He had chased that down with a generous jug of ale. He hadn't seen Rose since she served him his meal so he got up to find her. 'Rose? Where are you, Rose? They've got a fiddler performing at the Sledge and Muck tonight.

Are you going to escort me, Rose? Where are you?'

Thomas searched the kitchen, the dining room and the stables but couldn't find her. He served himself another half jug of ale when he heard the front door creak open. He hid his jar under the counter. Rose entered with Mr Fullgrout.

'Rose?' Thomas asked. 'Why are you with Mr Fullgrout?'

Before Thomas could answer, Mr Fullgrout approached Thomas with his hands behind his back and regarded him like a gust of foul air. 'I've soiled my boots to arrive here on a matter of *theft*, Mr Crown.'

'Theft, Mr Fullgrout? I don't know anything about any theft.'

'A *liar* as well as a thief!' Mr Fullgrout raised his voice. 'We have the evidence.'

Thomas shook his head. 'What evidence, Mr Fullgrout? There's no thievery occurring underneath this roof.'

From behind her back, Rose presented the fish bones to her husband. She couldn't resist a grin.

'Three pikes went missing from Mr Cornbuckon's fishery yesterday,' Mr Fullgrout revealed. 'If my nose is a reliable guide, your *wife* is holding up the very bones of those missing fish.'

Thomas gazed at Rose with disbelief. He shook his head once more.

'You know the customary punishment, Mr Crown,' Mr Fullgrout said with no little amount of pleasure. 'Or, you can spend the week in Bridewell prison. As you know the rats, skunks and badgers are not too friendly there. Your choice?'

Thomas swapped fierce glances with Rose before answering the magistrate. 'I'll take the customary punishment.

The next Saturday morning, Thomas's head, hands and feet were placed into wooden stocks in the market square by Mr Fullgrouts's assistants. Spoiled tomatoes in hand, Rose fronted the baying mob of mostly womenfolk. Again, spectators sat atop buildings and hung from chimneys for a better view. Mr Fullgrout raised his right arm. 'For the unspeakably foul and devilish crime of pilfering fish! Not one, not two but *three*. I sentence you for a pelting at leisure by the good people of Kingston!'

Rose was the first to launch her missile. It struck Thomas flush on his right cheek. All manner of rotten fruit and vegetables splat Thomas' face. The crowd roared and chuckled in delight.

A window opened on the first floor of the Seven Kings and Ham Inn. Mr Dickens surveyed the wild and boisterous scenes below him. He smiled as he wrote something in his notebook.

My City
—SUSAN HODGETTS

My city is not like other cities. Sure, it has sky scrapers and coffee shops, but this city is where my heart is. Jake, the one-armed ferryman (with the tattoo of a wild-eyed woman) cannot be found in Lisbon, or Copenhagen. Jake, who rows me to Ham each morning, in a handful of minutes. I like to watch the bulge of his arm as he pulls the single oar toward him, and then away, rowing first on his left, and then to his right, to manage a straight line. His muscle pops like corn. Jake likes tapioca, and watching wrestling—though not together. He eats in silence on his house-boat, to the sound of the waves. (He swears it's the only music he can bear). We talk of Dickens, but not of war. He lost his arm in service to the Royal Navy, abroad. Sometimes of an evening, we chase the moon across the water, glimpse a silent heron bent in shadow. We watch regal flotillas of Canada geese, and wake to the coo of pigeons in the early hours, after we have made love. Often I am the only one in the little wooden boat, at 8AM, though I sometimes share the 5PM return with day trippers. But I don't mind that, when I remember his heart beat, alone in the dark. And when I paint in my studio on long summer days, I think of him tanning on the deck. The hand-rowed ferry is a dying art, but in this city, people are still at its heart.

Guardian Angels
—ROBERT MCCANN

It is night and the Thames cuts a dark path through the orange sodium lamp glow, east of the city. Its unusual blackness swallows the reflections tonight and it pulls at my soul. I am drawn closer as I fight the alcohol fuzz in my head. The blur tells me the water is flat and I feel like I am looking deep into the pupil of a cold eye. The sense I have is of the blackness being a thing yet nothing you can touch. A black hole whose secrets elude until you step in. I move my scuffed leather shoe forward and feel the damp from the concrete soak through a hole and into my sock. As I go deeper the ice cold is apparent and I become aware of tidal sounds that belie the flatness.

Eight hours before it was the usual Friday after work lock in. Out came the wine and spirits in plastic tumblers, off came the work clothes, almost all the clothes in Gabby's case, as she unashamedly peeled her tights off, singing raucously, in the middle of the office floor like a child. All with the blinds up and visible from the street and all before she'd touched a drop of booze. Dan came back from the bathroom, in an even tighter outfit than his work suit and more make up on than the girls. I have never changed for a night out. Sandy emerged a goddess, seeming not to notice my stare.

Later, at the club, once carnage had descended to replace inhibition it struck me how alone I felt, yet posing for a photo with Gabby sat on my left thigh, Sandy on my right, both with arms draped round me, the three of us toasting with our shots.

My right foot is soaking. I shiver as the world spins. My body isn't cold on the outside.

I remember drinking and dancing and having fun. I remember feeling hopeless and despair. I don't remember anything between. I looked around and wanted to leave the club. On my own. I am thirty five and still don't tell people things. There isn't any point. Everyone loses their loved ones. Everything will be OK. We are all alone. I'm not unhappy but I can swim and keep going until everything stops. Just swim. Not stop.

'Hello?'

A woman's voice a distance behind.

'Are you alright?' she sounds concerned.

I lift and turn my head. There is grass and an empty square with trees bathed in orange. A block of flats behind. Quiet, lights off. Still. No-one there.

I climb the steps back onto the path. All quiet.

'Hello?' I shout.

No reply. No-one.

And I walk. Just walk. Not stop.

Silence Please
—ROGER DEAN

'How long are we supposed to stay here dad?' ten year old Ben asked his father, Bill.

'All morning, now do you see that sign hanging up over there?' Bill replied, severely as he pointed.

'Yeah?'

'Read it out to me.'

'S-I-L-E-N-C-E…P-L-E-A-S-E. Silence please.'

'Exactly and do you see those two burly uniformed attendants standing there directly under that sign?'

'Yeah?'

'Well they are here to make sure you do so I don't want to hear another peep out of you, have you got that?'

'Yeah.' Ben sighed to himself miserably.

It was the first day of the school summer holidays. He could have been out playing football with his mates but his dad had decided that it would be a good for them to visit the library and sit at this table and read boring books. His father had given him a book about the Kings and Queens of England. Ben would have preferred to sit at home and read his Beano. He had a copy in his inside jacket pocket but his dad would never let him read that here.

I might just as well be back at school. Ben thought to himself. Still at least he had his packet of boiled sweets with him to cheer him up. He decided to have one now.

Rustle! Rustle! Rustle! Rustle!

'What on earth are you doing boy?' Bill snapped irritably at him.

'Just having a sweet, dad. Would you like one?'

'No I wouldn't! If you have to eat sweets then empty them out of that noisy bag onto the table and do it…'

Clatter! Clatter! Clatter! Clatter!

'…quietly.'

'Sorry dad.'

'Just keep quiet, will you? I'm trying to read.'

'Okay.' Ben replied as he popped a sweet into his mouth.

Crunch! Crunch! Crunch! Crunch!

'Ben, you're making too much noise. Don't crunch your sweets like that. Suck them.'

'Okay dad.'

Slurp! Slurp! Slurp! Slurp!

That was when Bill really lost his temper with him as he banged his book on the table.

'QUIET BEN!!!!!!!!!! SHUT UP!!!!!!!!!!!!!!!!'

Just then the two attendants glanced at each other and nodded as they made their way over to their table.

'Now see what you've done. The attendants are coming over to throw you out now.'

Fine by me. I never wanted to come here in the first place. Ben thought to himself.

But to their surprise, the attendants grabbed hold of Bill.

'Here…what the…' Bill spluttered, in disbelief.

'Now come on sir, I'm afraid you will have to leave. You're causing a disturbance.' One of the attendants said.

'Yes but I…I…'

'Ha! Ha! You were making more noise than me trying to shut me up.' Ben laughed, as they frog marched his father out of the library and dumped him unceremoniously onto the street outside.

Ben then threw his book to one side, pulled out his Beano and popped another sweet into his mouth.

Perhaps this morning wasn't going to be so bad after all. Ben thought to himself.

Midday Dave
—DAVID BOTTOMLEY

The Irish landlord serves our halves of bitter and upon enquiry of the date of the distinctive oak interior, tells us 'It was refurbished completely in about 2005. It was just a shell, since it was flooded with the river, so it had to be all gutted and started again.' He points to the exterior fireplace wall, 'That wall behind you was only held up by the scaffolding!' The Angel pub at Rotherhithe occupies an enviable riverside corner plot, once end of a terrace, now the last man standing.

In a small back room overlooking the Thames, an old man is sat in the window seat steadily gazing out over the city. A dangerous looking Bunsen burner contraption is shooting flames into a Victorian style cast iron grate prepared with wood and coal.

'It blows hot air' he says in his cockney accent, 'like the missus' laughing his head off.

'This your local then?' I ask.

He thinks for a moment. 'Well you could say that. I call this my office, for my business affairs, mainly gambling. There's all my papers up there' pointing to a shelf in the alcove above him, 'When it's not that, I call it my front room!'

'Everybody knows where to find me. I've got fucking loads of grand daughters now and they come and see me in here, so there's no escape.

They call me 'Midday Dave', 'cause I can always be found in here at midday.

I've been coming in here about thirty year. I can remember it before it was refurbished. It was a Cameron's pub when I first came then a Trust House Forte before the present owner took it over.

But he knows what he's doing; he likes the old traditional style and that. There's no music, no TV's and no personal stereos, mobile phones. He keeps it like a proper old-fashioned boozer. That's what I like about it.

This gets full of walkers in the summer, when the old current bun's out. You get all these troops, these old women, look like they're on their last legs but they're ruthless old birds, you know- determined to do the whole bloody length. They go all down this side then they cross over the river and do Wapping and up back along Embankment.

Some people, they do these guided walks you know, 'tour guides', they spend an hour and a half online swatting up the night before then they come down and start telling everyone all about it. There's one guy last summer, came did all that, lives in Oxford, Oxford! He's got an office somewhere in the city, which he uses as a base and for his correspondence but he lives in Oxford!'

With that he puts an old woolly hat on his bald head and gets a rolly ready to go and smoke on the balcony outside, leaving a pile of lose coins on the table and his things, trusting that no one dare chance it.

On the Bridge
—FARHANA KHALIQUE

'Did you know that this is the only bridge in Britain with a church at each end?'

We were walking across Putney Bridge, but Michael had stopped halfway to point.

I said, 'Unless you're a vampire, I wouldn't worry.'

'Vampires are fine with churches,' he said. 'If they don't go in.'

I stared.

'Come on, Priya,' he said. 'Consecrated ground, crosses, holy water…?'

'You're such a weirdo,' I teased.

His laugh leaped above the buzz of traffic behind us.

He'd been doing that a lot lately. Commenting on churches, and temples. On white dresses and red lengas. On cakes and laddoos. He'd even threatened to take me to Paris recently, but I'd said I wasn't free.

'Shall we go?' I said.

'Oh, we're already late.' He waved a hand. 'Let's be tourists.'

I stopped myself from looking at my watch. We were facing upstream and I followed his gaze. Swathes of grey shifted overhead and pinpricks of rain began to fall. A couple of boats hovered by the sheds and one crept past, below us. Swirls and eddies danced around each other in its wake and the water tossed snakes of silt.

Fearing the frizz, I pulled up the hood of my jacket, but Michael leaned forward. His brown curls and pale cheeks glistened.

'It never stops, does it?' he said. 'Just wrinkles by one moment, then rushes the next.'

'Or you could go back a few hundred winters and go to skating on it.'

'That would be awesome!'

'If you say so.' I shivered theatrically.

He grabbed me and rubbed my shoulders and arms, and I giggled. Then I looked at him and waited.

He sighed and stepped back. 'Okay, Miss Boatspotter. Let's go.' He turned to the large Thai Square building that sprouted behind the pier.

'You don't mind do you?' I blurted.

He turned back, eyebrows raised. 'Why? I like your friends.'

'They're your friends too,' I said, but my voice was a fraud. Or, maybe I didn't want to convince him. Provoke, perhaps. Get a reaction, so that I wouldn't have to give one.

He eyed me. 'Well, I can't say I wouldn't rather have you all to myself this evening. But birthdays are fun. Celebrations are important.'

It was the way he said 'celebrations'. Trying not to taste it. Like a cake that he wasn't allowed to cut.

I gazed back at him. So smiley, yet so still. And I knew that it was because of me. Because I hadn't built that last bridge. Because I still hadn't told my parents that we were living together.

I stepped forward and looked up at him, foreheads and noses almost touching. 'They are important,' I murmured. 'Soon. I'll tell them soon.'

I closed my eyes, so that I wouldn't see if he believed me.

Ghosts of Brixton
—SANDRA WAREHAM

Whether Marcia was asleep or awake, Charlene's plan was to enter *the room* with exaggerated joviality and frivolity.

'No blasted way is my good friend to have any idea that she is soon to depart from this world...I'M NOT giving in to nauseating sombreness...We will reminisce and just buss some tunes on my phone.'

But regardless of her plan, Charlene's throat tightened at the thought of coming face to face with the dying.

The plan was to reminisce about bunking school and going to the Gambling Houses on *'The Line'* to buy a two-pound draw wrapped in bookie shop paper. The Gambling Houses that were saturated with the smell of fresh and stale ganja smoke, the smell of urine mixed with brandy, the sound of dominoes slamming down on rickety tables followed by the odd *'Bumberclaat'*, the shifty eyes of the hardcore card players, gold that decorated men of varying shades of black, in their teeth, on their fingers, dangling from a gallery of wrists and necks, like Ashanti Kings. *'The Stylers'*, in their Beaver hats, Cecil G sweaters, Farah trousers and Bally shoes in Croc, Alligator and Snake Skins, gave the old, near derelict, Victorian houses glamour, despite being long forgotten by the council.

'Marcia, do you remember rolling our first spliff? How, after sticking the five Rizla papers together the thing would fall apart at the seams after a few puffs. Flames burning up holes in our school uniforms, but nevertheless, was enough to have us in giggles that would continue for hours. How we would cough and laugh at our 'charge up' red eyes. Then hunger would 'tek we'

and we would raid your mum's cupboard and fry dumplings that we would chew on for what seem like hours... Marce... don't worry, ah goin' drap some tune fe yuh todeh, ALL your favourites, Louisa Marks, Dennis Brown, Janet Kay, Gregory, ah WHOLE-HEAP of Lovers Rock.'

Charlene smiled to herself as she remembered the shobeens hidden around Brixton, Harlesden and Dalston, their loyalty to *'Frontline Sound system'*, and how they sabotaged their books, school toilets and public spaces with the slogan *'Frontline sound ah de A1 Sound.'*

As the Nurse directed Charlene to the room, her sweaty hands had already moistened the wrapper that contained the mauve Carnations. Her throat constricted, her breaths quickened as they became shallow and sharp, almost gasping. Pressure began to build up behind her eyes and defined lines became blurry. She roughly cleared her throat so that the sensation vibrated throughout her body.

'Can't fail her now, this isn't what she would expect from me.'

Upon entering the room, and dismissing the image of a body that disintegrated into the bedding, almost impossible to distinguish between the gathered sheets or actual flesh, Charlene walked towards the smiling face doing *'de Bogle Dance' singing* ...*'Ting a ling ah ling, school bell ah ring, knife an' fark ah fight fi dumpling—bouyaka bouyaka Shabba Ranks 'im ah sing'...*

We Have More in Common Than Divides Us

—JUDE MCGOWAN

Len was in the local park dressed in a freshly ironed shirt and neat grey trousers when he nostalgically looked at the area that used to be a bowling green, now replaced by a children's maize. He thought to himself *they give too much to kids these days*. A little fair-haired girl came over to him and confidentially said 'why don't you come to my birthday party tomorrow? I don't have a grandad and I want one like my friend Josh'. He just said 'your Mum wouldn't like you talking to strangers'. Lucy was insistent and said it again. Lucy's Mum Sarah called several times to Lucy but she took no notice. Sarah came over to Len and said what a lovely sunny day it was, and when she heard Lucy for the third time asking Len to come to her party she said 'why don't you join us you only live at the other end of Manor Park? We live at no 22 so do come along'. Len wanted to say yes but he didn't know how. He had dismissed the invitation thinking *they don't want me cluttering up the place*, but the next day he decided he would go. Kids played happily on the scrubby grass and Lucy loudly proclaimed Len as her granddad as soon as he arrived. Sarah gently reminded Lucy that he wasn't her granddad, but would be a nice friend for them both and they would call him Len. Towards the end of the party Sarah explained that Lucy had no grandparents and that made her sad. She also apologised for the state of the garden but that she didn't have any time or money to improve it. Before he had realised he had offered to help with the garden 'that is as long as your husband doesn't mind'. I'm on my own Len so the offer is gratefully accepted.

Every Sunday morning he took his tools and worked on their garden. He was beginning to transform the garden and Lucy and Sarah loved his visits. In her head Lucy always thought of him as her granddad but called him Len. A year passed and Len still visited regularly and the garden didn't require so much work just to keep it ship shape. They were all sitting in the garden enjoying the space and the friendship when Lucy said 'Grandad would you help me with this puzzle' and Mum didn't say a word about calling him Len.

Responsibility

—RASHPAL BAGAL

As he looked into the mirror he observed an unrecognisable con-torted face, his eyes red and his normally clean shaven face dark with shadow. He walked away slowly. He didn't understand that which he had become, his moral compass lost. What on earth was north anyway? As he turned his head he caught the mere glimpse of a man in uniform before something struck him with brute force. He was unconscious.

She smiled at the driver as she boarded the bus, her green eyes dancing, mesmerising and hypnotic. The man behind her be-rated the driver for ignoring him as finally he was acknowledged. Sitting, she pulled the file from her bag and opened it with care, as she glanced down and examined the photo her lips curled. She pushed everything back into her bag. Still smiling, she felt a stabbing sensation building but she would not let it show.

He stared at the door, it was certainly solid. He would fail to break it despite his formidable strength. The red light above the entrance lit up and with an instant recognition his body pushed hard against the wall, anticipating the suffering he knew would certainly follow. As he recoiled, the door opened and his jaw locked wide open as he fixated on the image before him.

She walked past the guard and approached a weathered older gentleman sitting at a desk that seemed too large for his needs.

'Anything else I need to know?' she enquired with a submis-siveness that was rarely seen.

'No. Are you sure you are up to this?' his tone was businesslike.

'I rarely make mistakes and when I do I …well I fix them.'

He nodded and she walked past him down the corridor.

Feeling her bag to make sure it was there she took a breath and opened the door. She walked in without hesitation.

'I am sorry!' he looked up and met her gaze as he spoke. She was silent. 'I didn't mean for things to turn out this way, truly. I love you more than anything, I couldn't have known that I would find you when I took this …job' She was silent still.

Her eyes darted left then right, emotions of longing and love rose up within her. She stepped forward and lowered herself to where he was chained. Her arms wrapped around him, holding him close as he pushed his head against hers. Images of Paris flew through her head as his mind felt his compass begin to chart its correct course once more.

The bullet made hardly a whisper of noise. He fell back in an almost poetic manner against the wall. She stood, took a moment to gather herself and wipe the small amount of blood that her perfectly aimed shot had allowed to land on her. Her mind now focused, she walked to the door and knocked. She smiled as she walked out but this time her eyes were not dancing.

Ritual

—ELAINE LOWE

Sleep was a welcome, comforting friend; it was Violet's only visitor. Her days were long and muddled, her memories were fragmented, like pieces of a jigsaw that somehow didn't fit. She did not resist when sleep slowly beckoned her, drawing her in and enveloping her to a place of calm and tranquillity, a place where she was safe. As her eyelids drooped, her darting mind would be still for a while.

Peacefulness washed over her as she drifted in to her slumber and she snuggled back into her chair. It was in the comfort of her dreams that Violet escaped the turmoil of the present and recalled the past with clarity.

The door of the lounge swung open as Violet's sister Rose came barrelling through, carrying two cups of tea in her pudgy hands, slopping the contents in to the saucers as she put the cups down on the table beside Violet.

'Sleeping and smiling Vi, that must be some dream you're having.' She chuckled in her deep, croaky, forty a day voice.

Violet woke completely disorientated; she began to pull out hair rollers ferociously, leaving little rigid curls like brandy snaps on her head.

'My lipstick, I can't find it!' She screeches, 'I have to get ready, they'll be here in a minute.' Violet cries as she rummages around in her old battered pink vanity bag.

Rose shakes her head in dismay at Violet's outburst, although she was used to it, she still found it upsetting.

It was the same every day. Violet would get ready, expecting visitors that had long since passed away. She would retreat back to decades ago when she and Rose were young and relish in reliving their wonderful past

Rose didn't remember their past in quite the same way. She was always waiting. Waiting to grow up, waiting to work with Violet in the factory. Waiting to marry Sidney and then more time wasted, waiting for him to come home drunk and penniless. He was gone now, God rest him. Rose was done with waiting.

Rose looked over at Violet, who was now sniffing a bottle of setting lotion. 'Do you remember that green stuff we used to get our beehive hairdo just right? What was it called?' Violet asked.

'Amami, it was called Amami Vi.' Rose replied.

Violet's face lit up as she remembered another little gem from the past, 'Do you remember that night we went to the pictures with those boys? And Dad was so angry with us for coming back late, he was pacing up and down the street his face purple with rage.'

Rose laughed loudly, 'Yeah and when he saw us come round the corner he started tapping his watch.'

They both chuckled.

'Let's not wait in today, why don't we go to the pub' Rose said.

'Does it still shut at 10.30?' Violet asked as she swiped a stub 'Tangerine Dream' across her lips.

My Story
—JOHN LEWIS

My story begins, when one day; I woke up in a hospital bed. I had no idea how I had got there or where there even was. I couldn't ask the other patients because they all appeared to be permanently asleep. My voice was muffled and weak and I didn't seem able to attract the attention of the nurses, who I believed were the large white blobs that were moving about in the distance. I tried to recollect what had happened to me in the recent past, as I thought that this would explain my present situation.

What did I know? I knew that my name was Ernest Jones. I knew that I was a librarian. I knew that I worked for a section of the British Secret Service and the last thing I remembered was that it was 1953 and I was going on holiday. I should not have gone on holiday. They had made me go.

They said that I was spending too much time at work and that I needed to take time off. They had hinted that some of my behaviour was bordering on the obsessive. I remembered how much I disliked the users of the library and their creepy desire to borrow or even handle the books I held in my care. I was trying to keep the knowledge of the ancient's safe, for that brief period called the present, when I was its guardian. Scrolls that were made using the skins of animals and books bound in their author's flesh, proper books, not the mass produced rubbish that people today think of as literature, histories of the civilisations that existed before the flood, before Adam and Eve.

I wondered whether it was still 1953. I remembered that 1953 was the year that felt like the country had finally been given a fresh start. Rationing had ended and we had witnessed the coronation of our new monarch, on our newly purchased black and white television sets. Churchill was Prime Minister again and the country, though still broke, appeared to be coming back to life. The war that had started in 1939 had finally ended.

Despite these signs of renewal, I'd noticed a lot of damaged people wandering the streets of London. Men who had been deeply traumatised by the war, whose wounds although not visible, would blight the rest of their lives and lonely men and women, who having lost or misplaced their families during the blitz, now had no real connection to the world. Some of the men after being demobbed either did not want to go back home or had no homes to go back to and you could see them wandering the streets in their frayed and ragged demob suits, as they slowly started to turn into tramps. I remembered thinking that sometimes you did not need to be dead to be a ghost and that there were a lot of ghosts wandering the streets of London in 1953.

The Streets of London
—LINDA MUNDY

It was a beautiful sunny morning as Cathy packed the car, ready for her journey to work. Handbag, laptop, gym kit and one extra bag today. She turned the radio on, opened the windows and took in a deep breath of fresh country air. As she passed the Village Hall, a sign reminded her of the Summer Fete on Saturday.

On approaching the motorway, she wondered what kind of response she would get from Nick later that evening when they met for a drink as usual before she went to Pilates.

They'd called it their 'Drink and Debate Date'. Cathy often had to dash off just as they were at a crucial point of discussion. Sometimes they had a quick chat again on her way back, but more often than not Nick had settled for an early night.

Cathy's journey was going well, but as she left the motorway, she felt a little uneasy about seeing Nick this week, hoping he would not be cross with her. She had been gently dropping hints for a while now, but was a little more direct last week when she told him that he really ought to get some new trousers. The pair he was wearing had seen better days, so she decided to buy a pair for him. There were some very formal ones in the shop which looked really nice, but that was definitely not Nick's style.

She turned up the volume to her favourite song, 'Streets of London', and sang loudly, 'So how can you tell me, your L O N E L Y, and say for you that the sun don't shine…' The sun was certainly shining today, but she quickly closed the windows and put on the air conditioning rather than breathing in the polluted dirty air in the city.

After work, she walked along to meet Nick, and took in the mixture of smells—dirty pavements as it had not rained for ages, kebabs, curries, fish and chips and pungent spices from the vegetable stalls.

While they were chatting, Cathy felt anxious about broaching the subject of his trousers again, so left it until about five minutes before her class was due to start before passing them to him.

Nick was a bit off-hand with her, saying she shouldn't have bought them, but Cathy said they didn't cost much and had left the receipt in the bag for him to see. She hoped they would fit.

Nick pulled the trousers out of the bag, along with the receipt—£2.50 cash paid in a charity shop. He did not mind so much now and gave her a grin.

As she started to walk off, she said 'You are not offended are you?' Nick said 'No, I'm not offended but I can't wear them—they are navy, I only wear brown'.

Cathy replied 'Nick—you are so unreal'!!

She patted his dog and, as usual, put some loose change in Nick's hat on the ground before leaving.

Candy
—SARA HAFEEZ

Lucas was thinking about his little girls. He hadn't lived with
them and their mother pretty much since they were babies. In his
mind's eye, they are dancing in one of the many birthday parties
he went to as a child in the 80s. They're wearing matching patent
white shoes and they have their hair crimped like the girls who
used to chase him round the mobile-disco lit town halls and
scout huts of suburbia. Somehow he always imagines them in
memories from his own childhood.

He felt a plasticky squelch under his trainer and saw lumpen
chewing gum, festering there, moist in the dry grass. A sticky
reminder that this was not the time for ambling through his
thoughts and taking in the afternoon sun. It was a sticky reminder
that despite the bustling mass moving along the snack stalls, he
had to find candy floss for his girls.

He had left them with his brother. He had left them singing her
the theme tune from that thing they're obsessed with, as Martin
looked on bemused. He knew he didn't have much time. His eyes
followed a gaggle of kids forcing the pink stuff into their mouths.

He approached the sweaty crowd and despaired. Mothers,
aunties, big sisters in the scrum were not just jostling, but active-
ly competing for the front of the queue. He looked skywards and
exhaled slowly. He pictures the girls on a bus home from school,
swapping stickers and getting irritated about the doubles that
they don't have. Sasha starts to bait Sana, who's getting angrier
and shoutier with each character her sister screams the name of.
Red faced, Sana flips out. A face is slapped.

Get a grip, man! He was losing this battle. Surveying the throng once more, he tried to make an inroad, he tried to twinkle his eyes at soft-lashed or apple cheeked young women, but no one holds his gaze, no response. Who are these people?

My babies! For my babies!

No one hears his exclamations. Hand gestures, pleading looks all fall on deaf ears, not so much English was being spoken, it seemed. He looked out to the marquees on the far side of the green. They seemed like bedsheets fashioned into makeshift dens on rainy days. He sees the girls playing in tiny box-shaped living room, their blonde-brown hair plaited tightly in a single low braid on each of them. They are crawling under the skinny legged plastic chairs and pulling his mother's long white skirts and plain white sari fabric over them, he can hear her laughing and chasing them round, scooping them up, putting them on her lap, before their heads rest in the curves of her neck, while she hums a song in a language they don't know.

Lucas stopped, suddenly certain he can hear crying. As the sounds of families around him resurface into the school fair hubbub, he is completely alone.

Eau de Chat
—ELISABETH GUSS

I woke up this morning and discovered that I'd lost my sense of humour. Everything annoyed me. I felt like one of those grouchy old women on that TV program. I searched for it beneath the sofa. It wasn't there. It wasn't in the bedroom either where my husband was snoring softly. I looked into the garden and that may have been the problem.

My radiant oleander bush from Corsica had disappeared. So had the olive tree from Greece. The espaliered fig only held hard, dry spheres and even this was leaving; its branches laden with ripe fruit had stretched across the wall into the sunny garden next door.

This neighbour didn't even want my figs. She had her own preferred tastes: crab-apple jelly, elderberry wine and quince. Peering around my garden I detected things were even worse.

The untrimmed bay, left to itself, had spread its canopy monstrously above my little London rainforest, choking off what light remained since the neighbour opposite received approval to build upward. I realised then, that the magnolia hadn't flowered this year and the grandiflora which had never flowered, possibly because it was a male and had not female nearby with which to mate—or is it the reverse? Who can afford a gardening expert in these lean years of austerity?

And the final tragedy that I beheld, was my eucalyptus. Inspired by the literary work of the Australian writer, BLANK, I'd had such hopes for this poor tree. It had endured for nearly twenty years despite Blighty's dearth of sunshine, inclement hale and rainstorms. But sometime since I'd last ventured out into the garden, had chosen to expire. Had given up the ghost.

Fittingly, it looked like the ghost of a tree: whitish, weightless, quite dry, it was a log leaning against the house, and my wild bengal cats were walking along it, higher and higher to the upper storeys. And who was looking down from the third floor but my crazy young and stylish friend from Oxford, of whom I am quite fond, Oscar.

My husband and I were witnesses at his town hall marriage to an Estonian boyfriend. He can't have noticed me because as he stood there by his open window he proceeded to piss slowly down into the garden for what must have been the umpteenth time and I realised I'd unearthed the source of the peculiar smell we'd been wondering about: a smell my husband insisted was male urine and, not knowing better, I'd called eau de chat.

Then my sense of humour returned and I burst out laughing.

There be Dragons
—ALISON CATCHPOLE

The city lay quiet. Tired workers were tucked up. Children were dreaming. A dream shaping their imagination, though their parents would tell them it was the other way around. They went to sleep with one horizon. Those who awoke would awake with another.

The city lay quiet.

And then, it didn't.

People had forgotten how to tend a dragon, or how to feed it. While the dragon had been dormant, the city had grown, but grown apart. It had forgotten how to appease its hidden residents. So the rumour was that they didn't exist.

They used to be marked by apprehensive mapmakers, 'There Be Dragons'. Unknown dangers were lurking, so they named them. But when the dragons slunk away, tired and replete, so did their memory. Gradually everyone forgot about them. Out of sight, out of mind.

Then there was a hot summer. There had been rumours of a resurfacing. People had protested, but hadn't been heard. It wasn't clear if they hadn't found the right words, or if the right words hadn't found the right people, or indeed, if the right people had found the right people. The nature of right had become confused—what, after all, was right? Was it old? New? Safer? Safest?

For some time, people had tried to fight for better dragon proofing. 'If it happens, though,' the authorities had argued, 'we've taken measures'. They'd stopped sleeping some time ago, so they'd stopped dreaming. Which of course meant they'd stopped having the imagination maintenance they so badly needed.

The essence rose. It rose, by any other name; by any other name it excited, expanded and skittered into life. At first, there was no rightness or wrongness, just an essence, stirring, igniting; growing.

It was the light that people noticed first. 'Look,' said one. 'It's on fire. That building's on fire. You can taste it in the air. Listen!'

And you could. Ashen chunks of fertile building material fell through the air. Smoke filled people's lungs and drowned them in their own mortality.

There was no anger like it.

The dragon tamers, stretched taut across the skies, nearly snapped. Men and women in hard yellow helmets were almost melting in the breath of the terrible creature. They knew beasts, but even they had no idea how to frighten this one. Taming was out of the question, and that was what they'd been trained in. After all, people had stopped believing in dragons.

Hindsight was, as always, twenty-twenty, or thereabouts. The flames had been conquered and of course, when the daylight came, no one talked of dragons any more. Dragons, after all, didn't exist. They couldn't be seen or heard, so that proved it.

Rising from ashes, the people waved and begged for help. Through closed eyes they screamed.

The unreality had moved one step closer. The nightmare was the reality.

We are alive. We continue without our belongings, without our families.

People decided they wouldn't forget. They wouldn't want to. They couldn't anyway.

The Day Mum Won The Lottery

—ELIZABETH SHODA

One day, my mum, who is always miserable and hardly ever leaves her room, ran into my bedroom and cried, 'We won the lottery!' She picked me up and hugged me. Her nightgown smelled of wet dogs. 'Don't tell anyone,' Mum warned. 'Some people would kill for money.' I promised not to tell a soul. I did not want to lose my mum.

That week, I wrote down all the things I'd spend the money on. I wished Mum would check my spelling. Instead, she stayed in her room and spent the entire day singing. At least she wasn't miserable, but her singing was very loud. Sometimes she would sing so loud, I hardly got any sleep. Then Miss Jenkins, after catching me sleeping in class, would punish me by asking me to read the longest word on the board.

A month went by, and still, no sign of the money. Then one day, Mum stopped singing and she called me into her room. 'Our neighbour found out about the money!' she sobbed. 'Now he is threatening me!' I ran to my mum and held her, while on the other side of the wall, the angry man banged his fist and shouted the F-word. 'This is my last warning! Otherwise, I'll come over and stuff a sock down your throat!' he yelled before it went silent. I was very sacred because Mum was right. Some people would kill for money.

The next day, Miss Jenkins told me to make my way to the head teacher's office. I had no idea why. I had not fallen asleep. When I arrived, there were two policemen. I burst into tears.

'The man next door killed my mum, didn't he?' I cried. The policemen looked confused. They said our neighbour was disturbed by Mum's loud singing and decided to call the police. But once they arrived, they realised Mum was not very well. I was told to follow them to their police car. I didn't understand what was happening. If Mum was unwell, then why did the police, and not the doctor, show up at my school? It must have been a trick. To get me to tell them about the money. But I promised Mum I would not tell a soul. And a soul I would not tell.

We arrived at a small building, a bit like the place Mum took me when I had chicken-pox. This wasn't a hospital! How dare they try to fool me! Later, they sat me in a room in front of a friendly-looking woman. She said she was a social worker. She began to ask me questions, shoving a biscuit under my nose. Social! Yeah right! She too was after the money. So, I kept quiet, stared at her clipboard, and spelled out, in my head, the long word on top: s-c-h-i-z-o-p-h-r-e-n-i-a.

If only I could read.

Brioche
—YVONNE BOWDEN

I bought some brioche swirls and strong Italian coffee. I also bought pears and lots of vegetables because he didn't eat meat unless it was halal. I bought food which I thought he would like. I bought food which I hoped he would eat.

When I got to the station he was already there. He looked tired and dirty and his cream puffa jacket was covered in stains and was torn. He had been so proud of his jacket. The last time I saw him it was new. I felt sad to see him like that. We jumped on a train and then he said he wanted to get off, just like that. I was afraid of losing him again so I followed him off the train. It was getting quite late and I told him we needed to get back. He lay down in the park. He was tired he said and hadn't slept for days. He took off his shoes and I noticed that his socks were full of holes. I told him to throw them away and he did. His perfect feet were so dirty.

There we were in the middle of nowhere. The last train had gone. We started to walk aimlessly but we managed to hitch a lift. A middle-aged woman pulled up in an old Renault 4. There were two sullen teenagers sitting in the back. She'd been to see her daughter who was married to a foreigner who had the same accent as me. Did I come from the same place she said.

When we arrived home he didn't want to come in but he did. He slept and he showered and he ate. We watched movies on a mini iPad. Sometimes I went out to buy food and he stayed at home. The days rolled by and then it was Sunday.

'What are you going to do?' I said. He said he didn't know that he wanted to stay with me but I said he couldn't. He told me he had an appointment but he didn't see the point in going. I agreed with him. I said he couldn't stay here in this country he would be picked up by the police. I bought him a ticket to L. He lay in my arms sobbing quietly. Then it was time to go.

I could feel that he didn't want to get on the coach but he did and he never waved goodbye. We knew that we would never see each other again. He rang me a few days later and asked me to meet him under the clock tower. He said he would wait for me until 10PM. I didn't go. I wanted to go.

I think of him every day and sometimes I think I may have seen him in the park or on the train but it's not him. I wonder what he looks like now? 10 years older. Perhaps he has a wife and kids. Perhaps not. Who knows.

The Meeting
—TAMARA GALLOWAY

The wall is a deep orange colour. Whatever else changes in the neighbourhood, it remains the same. Many of the bricks have their surface gouged out, by someone who must have been very frustrated. It seems solid and hasn't required repair all these years. It sometimes gets decorated with beer glasses or bottles.

There are rich pickings around here. I can usually find tasty morsels or choice titbits. There's a kebab shop just across the road and when people walk up the hill they sometimes chuck nearly complete, person-sized meals onto the grass verge at the side of the pavement. That's a red-letter day for me. They're so stupid. Other times they throw crunchy chicken bones too. Those bins smell lovely. That wretched wall means I can't get to them though.

I've tried to get through one of the holes at the bottom of the beech hedge, so I can reach the bins the other way, but the caretaker at the school has put up wire netting so I can't get through there either. You can't imagine what torture it is, to be able to smell all that mouth-watering food, but not be able to get to it. Its perfume wafts out to me through the extractor fan of the pub kitchen.

People can just walk in there and eat it. I don't know why but they just let them have it, and they always seem to have more food coming. It's so much easier than having to catch small animals or birds whenever you want a snack. It's lovely and warm in there too. Once, in the depth of winter, I went inside.

They seemed so shocked to see me. 'Shoo!' and 'Get out!' was all I got, although the rain was pouring down outside, and I felt my tail was freezing off. They just don't know how lucky they are…

One night the smell was so lovely I just couldn't resist it. I was in the middle of crossing the road when suddenly this woman came round the corner. I was so surprized I just stopped dead, in the middle of the road, and stared at her.

She stopped too, and gazed at me, as though she'd never seen one before. 'How odd', I thought. 'People aren't usually up this late. What's she doing?'

'Awww' she said, 'I won't hurt you. Don't mind me.'

There was a distant rumble and a pair of headlights came round the corner.

'NO!!!' the woman yelled. I scarpered so quickly it made me feel quite nervous. 'There's no need to scare me like that,' I thought.

About the contributors

North London

BRENT

City of Stories Writer-in-Residence 2017: Bidisha
Bidisha is an author, journalist and BBC and Sky broadcaster. She also does outreach work in UK prisons, detention centres and refugees' resource centres. This inspired her fifth book, 'Asylum and Exile: Hidden Voices of London', which was published in 2015. She is a Trustee of the Booker Prize Foundation, looking after the UK's most prestigious literary prizes for fiction in English and in translation.

Winner: Elizabeth Uter
Elizabeth Uter has taught poetry workshops for Farrago Poetry and Kensington & Chelsea Library Services. Performance Poet at UK Slams & Festivals. Two short plays commissioned by The Actors' Centre & Barking & Dagenham Library Services. Published: SouthWestFest Magazine & Barking & Dagenham Poetry Anthology 2016.

Highly Commended: Kristel Tracey
Queen Nefertiti in a past life. Reborn in Luton as a pleb. Reinvented as a too-much-to-say-for-herself Londoner and aspiring writer.

Winner: Sinead Beverland
Passionate about storytelling, I'm a writer and Film graduate
living in South London. I blog about new discoveries, am penning
a collection of short stories and my first feature script is currently
in development.

Highly Commended: Charlotte Forfieh
Charlotte Forfieh lives in a Folkestone. She writes slipstream-y
short stories and screenplays—if it's a bit out there she's probably into it. She is currently studying an MA in creative writing at
Birkbeck, University of London as a Kit de Waal Scholar.

Highly Commended: Kim Horrocks
A single female northerner, with two babes in arms, who scurried
to London in the 80's to escape the rest of her life being held
back by old fashioned sexist values. Believes the Arts are the
only gateway to the truth of the human condition and the libera-
tion from oppression. Loves dogs more than humans. Has many
flaws. Cheeky.

Winner: Liam Hogan
Liam Hogan's twisted fantasy collection, 'Happy Ending Not Guaranteed', is published by Arachne Press. His award winning story, 'Ana', appears in Best of British Science Fiction 2016. He's often found on stage hosting Liars' League. Find out more at *happyendingnotguaranteed.blogspot.co.uk*

Highly Commended: Clare Palmer
Clare Palmer has been writing short stories for five years, and was published for the first time last December. As a family carer, much of her time is spent in learning disability training and activism. She lives in Islington.

Highly Commended: Pam Williams
I'm a fifty-something Londoner of Grenadian heritage; a former fashion journalist/stylist—now a trainee teacher. Creative writing was my secret love but I'm finally sharing my stories and performing my poetry and dream of touching people with my words.

Highly Commended: Andrés Ordorica
Andrés is a graduate of The Royal Central School of Speech & Drama. He is the 2016 Winner of the Bloomsbury Festival's Short Story Slam. He is passionate about sharing stories that reflect his world: queer, brown, beautiful and unapologetic.

East London

City of Stories Writer-in- Residence 2017: Courttia Newland
Courttia Newland is the author of seven works of fiction including his debut, The Scholar. He was nominated for the Impac
Dublin Literary Award, The Frank O' Conner award, The CWA
Dagger in the Library Award, The Hurston/Wright Legacy Award
and The Theatre 503 Award for playwriting as well as numerous
others. His short stories have appeared in many anthologies and
broadcast on BBC Radio 4. In 2016 her was awarded the Tayner
Barbers Award for science fiction writing and the Roland Rees
Busary for playwriting. He is associate lecturer in creative writing
at the University of Westminster and is completing a PhD in creative
writing. Courttia was City of Stories Writer-in-Residence 2017.

Winner: Danielle Higgins
Danielle Higgins is a local artist and lecturer who finds inspiration from the vibrant plentitude of birdlife, nature and communities within the Springfield and River Lea areas of Hackney. Danielle graduated with an MA in the history of art in 2013, and since then has creatively indulged in building a portfolio of illustrations accompanied by short stories that explore the theme of anthropomorphism. *daniellehiggins.co.uk*

Highly Commended: Anna Latimer
I discovered my love of writing late after a career as an artist, photographer and teacher. I have been writing for about five years and am currently working on a novel.

Highly Commended: Jon Fortgang
Jon is published by Galley Beggar Press and has been a winner/ finalist in prizes run by Writers & Artists, BritWriters and more. After a decade as a journalist, he now works in his local library where he helps run a writer's group. A novel is under construction.

Winner: Ruth Goldsmith

Ruth writes short stories when she's trying to find a constructive way of avoiding her work in progress. While she loves creating fiction, she finds it really, really difficult to write her own author bio.

Highly Commended: Lauren Miller

Lauren Miller performs her poetry and fiction regularly in London, and recently studied a masters in creative Writing at Birkbeck. Her work has been shortlisted for the Bridport Prize and Fish Poetry Prize, and in 2016 her short story 'Warm Feeling' was published in the anthology Mechanics Institute Review 13.

Highly Commended: Katherine Davey

I'm reader, a writer, and—for money!—an editor. I belong to the very wonderful writing group, Free Lunch, and along with words, I love people (some in particular), art, trees and birds.

Winner: Josephine Phillips
Born and bred in Canning Town. Have always worked. Am a committed and active member of WASPI. Enjoy reading, writing (one of the Rathbone Writers), local history, lots of walking and zumba/dance. Very opinionated, always have something to say.

Highly Commended: Julie Browne
I am 66, semi retired, I live alone very happily with my cat, I have many hobbies including knitting, crochet, sewing, studying Ancient Greek and growing tomatoes and chillis on my window sills. I love live theatre, fringe rather than the West End! I used to write when I was young, but life overtook me, so I am coming back to it afresh. I have loved being part of Rathbone Writers and hope to continue.

Highly Commended: Saundra Daniel
From my earliest memory, I have been surrounded by books, and since primary school, story—regardless of format—has been one my biggest writing influencers. I'm indebted to my parents who constantly encouraged creativity, open mindedness, and perseverance.

Winner: Anna James

Anna James lives in the borough of Redbridge, where she enjoys helping children to embrace their creativity and gain confidence as writers. She has studied Creative Writing at the University of East Anglia and loves to write about London.

Highly Commended: Harvinell Tatton

Harvinell is a children's librarian with a passion for storytelling and writing. Married with two sons, she believes her faith enables her to enjoy life and help others to do the same, by taking them on a literary adventure.

Highly Commended: Claire Baker

Since childhood I have loved creating stories that allow you to experience the joy and mystery of another world or another person's life. I belong to a writer's group where I regularly write short stories and poems.

Winner: Victoria Taylor

I am 46 and married with three children. I volunteer at my local library and attend a weekly writing group. I have written a book which I hope to publish soon and have another two in the planning stage. *victoriataylorauthor.com*

Highly Commended: Clare Vasiljevic

Clare Vasiljevic is a lover of words whether reading, writing, or eavesdropping on strangers conversations. Clare is working for a women's charity, raising her wildly energetic toddler and snatching moments in between on the bus and after midnight to write her second novel.

Highly Commended: Sharon Outten

My hobby is writing short stories. I have lived in the Borough of Barking and Dagenham since 1999 and really like living in this area very much and like to go to my creative writing group and attend creative writing events to get ideas to help me with my story writing.

South London

Winner: Janet Poaros

Born in Tunbridge Wells: lived in Kent, Dorset and then Cyprus with my late husband. Three children. Seven grandchildren. Taught ceramics in Cyprus & U.K. I enjoy designing/creating stories, gardens, recipes, artworks and ceramics: love reading, dancing, theatre, traveling.

Highly Commended: Mary Jupp

Studied creative writing with OU towards Humanities degree, then switched to Open College of The Arts to complete degree in CW. I write in a variety of genres and voices. This is my first published story and I'm delighted!

Highly Commended: Tony Clelford

Tony Clelford is finishing his novel about identity theft and media manipulation in a time of financial meltdown—set in 1720.

Highly Commended: Lorna McCook

Retired schoolteacher. Mother and grandmother with a keen interest in arts and crafts. Definite animal lover.

Winner: Aris Tsontzos

Aris Tsontzos is a database manager from London. He is an English graduate, a keen volunteer and a fan of talking about things and writing things down. He has always had a soft spot for stories.

Highly Commended: Han Smith

I am a writer, a reader, a teacher and a learner, currently quite interested in islands, tides and gender.

Highly Commended: Tom O'Brien

Tom writes short stories and flash fiction. He has been published in the Uncommon Lands, Blood & Bourbon. DEFY! and Blink Ink print anthologies and many places online.

City of Stories Writer-in- Residence 2017: Irenosen Okojie

Irenosen Okojie's debut novel, 'Butterfly Fish', won a Betty Trask Award and has been shortlisted for an Edinburgh International Book Festival First Book Award. Her short stories have been published internationally, including the Kwani 07 and Platitude. Her short story collection, 'Speak Gigantular', was published in 2016 and was shortlisted for the Jhalak Prize for writers of colour and longlisted for the Edge Hill Short Story Prize.

Winner: Aaron Cox

Aaron grew up in Sydney and has an MA in Creative Writing. His short stories have received commendations at the London Short Story Prize (2016), BBC Radio 4's Opening Lines and US journal Glimmer Train. He lives in London with his wife and two children.

Highly Commended: Yovanka Paquete Perdigao

Yovanka Paquete Perdigao is a Bissau-Guinean writer, editor and translator. Her poetry has been published in Brittle Paper, her translations in Jalada and her writing in the Guardian, English Pen and AFREADA.

Highly Commended: Simon Higgs

Professional gin drinker and library guy, but never at the same time. Wrote a novel three years ago and has been editing it ever since.

Highly Commended: Anita Goveas

Anita Goveas is British-Asian, based in London, and fueled by strong coffee and paneer jalfrezi. She was published in the 2016 London Short Story Prize anthology.

Winner: Vicky Richards

Vicky Richards moved to London two years ago from Shropshire. By day she edits children's non-fiction, and in her spare time she pretends to work on a historical fantasy novel.

Highly Commended: Lucinda Offer

Lucinda Offer is a keen amateur photographer and wildlife observer who can often be found exploring parks and anywhere with water. She is involved with community garden projects and a mental health charity in Croydon, where she lives.

Highly Commended: Lynne Couzins

It has been fifty years since I last entered a writing competition. The first was run by Jackanory when I was a child, I was disappointed that my story didn't win anything. This time I am happy!

Winner: Oksana Wenger

While trying to write a novel I realised I needed to translate my father's memoirs (into English), which I'm now hoping to publish. Concurrently I can't resist writing short stories but this is the first time I've actually won anything.

Highly Commended: Sophie Ronald

Sophie grew up in Surrey and moved to London after graduating from Nottingham University almost a decade ago. She now works at a media agency, and in her spare time enjoys music, writing, art and films.

Highly Commended: Joanne Gale

Jo is an actor. She has written and solo-published two children's picture books 'The Rare Monkey with the Colourful Bottom' and 'The Rare Monkey, Can't, Couldn't, Can!'

City of Stories Writer-in- Residence 2017: Alex Wheatle

Alex Wheatle was born in 1963. Alex spent most of his childhood in social services care. He is the author of novels including: 'Brixton Rock', 'East of Acre Lane', 'The Seven Sisters', 'Island Songs', 'Checkers', co-written with Mark Parham and 'The Dirty South'. Alex was awarded an MBE for services to literature in 2008. Alex's first young adult novel, 'Liccle Bit', was longlisted for the Carnegie Medal 2015. 'Shame & Scandal', Alex's debut play, played to sold out audiences at the Albany Theatre, Deptford in October, 2015. His Young Adult novel 'Crongton Knights' won the Guardian's Children's fiction award for 2016, the Renaissance Quiz Writers' Choice Award and has been shortlisted for the 2017 Bookseller Young Adult prize.'Straight Outta Crongton', the third in the Crongton trilogy, was published in April 2017.

Winner: Susan Hodgetts

Susan Hodgetts is an actor and playwright with a Masters' Degree in Writing for Performance. She has had plays produced at the Network Theatre and RADA.

Highly Commended: Robert McCann

Robert McCann works in aviation and enjoys running, swimming, writing, reading and fine art. He lives in South West London.

Highly Commended: Roger Dean

I'm 62 years old, I used to work as a finance officer for Kingston Council until I took the option of early retirement in April 2015. I have always enjoyed writing stories, mainly short stories but have completed some longer ones, over 400 pages. This will be the first time I will have anything in print so I'm honoured and delighted.

Winner: David Bottomley

David is Literary Manager of the Jack Studio Theatre, a playwright, poet and creative writing tutor. He has had plays produced in London, Edinburgh and America. Originally from Yorkshire, he has been resident documenting the landscape and characters of London for nineteen years.

Highly Commended: Farhana Khalique

Farhana Khalique is a teacher, voiceover and writer. She has been teaching English for over ten years, is often heard on TV as an announcer for Channel 4, and her stories have appeared in Carillon and The Asian Writer magazines.

Highly Commended: Sandra Wareham

I have been a Brixton resident all of my life. I have attended various creative writing workshops/courses (mainly within Lambeth). I enjoy writing about first generation West Indians and second generation Black British. I enjoy reading and World Cinema.

EALING

Winner: Jude McGowan

77 year old widow, two girls (Kate died in 1980). Worked in publishing / with children in care / older people now retired. A humanities degree in 1988. Supported a very disabled husband for ten years & now getting my life back together.

Highly Commended: Rashpal Bagal

Rashpal Bagal believes that the world is full of amazing stories. On the tube to work or watching the world while sipping coffee, tales are created in front of us. He wants to write many more of these stories.

HAMMERSMITH & FULHAM

Winner: Elaine Lowe

Elaine Lowe is a Bookseller at Pocketshop Hammersmith. Ritual is her first credited piece of work. She is an avid reader and her passion is travel whenever possible.

Highly Commended: John Lewis

I am 51 years old and I live in Shepherds Bush. I have self published a novel called 'The British Alien' on Amazon and I am hoping to write a follow up to it.

Highly Commended: Linda Mundy

Linda lives in West London and is married with two grown up children. She started to write short stories this year, and was delighted that this piece was Highly Commended. Her hobbies include reading, swimming and photography.

Winner: Sara Hafeez

I'm a librarian from South London. Always observing, learning, and writing.

Highly Commended: Elisabeth Guss

I've worked in publishing in the US, UK and France as a free-lance editor. Also in films in this country as a researcher/story editor. My education was in the US and I did graduate work in French at Stanford University. I moved to the UK in the sixties and have dual nationality. I was a single parent and my son is an artist concerned with human rights. My writing is unfinished, unedited and unpublished.

Highly Commended: Alison Catchpole

Alison arrived in London after reading Experimental Psychology at Oxford. Her subsequent teaching career has included state and independent schools in London and five years in Brussels. She has an MPhil in screenwriting and divides her time between W11 and Somerset.

Winner: Elizabeth Shoda

Elizabeth Shoda currently works for a cancer charity but dreams to be a full-time author. She is currently writing a Christian fiction novel she intends to finish by the end of the year.

Highly Commended: Yvonne Bowden

Born in London but have lived in France for many years. I have done all sorts of jobs since leaving school at 16. I have always loved writing. Love art. Love travelling.

Highly Commended: Tamara Galloway

Tamara Galloway was born, brought up and still lives in Orpington. She enjoys words, music and science.

She sees things through other creatures' eyes, becoming vegetarian at six, when she connected animals in fields and what was on her plate.

Acknowledgements

City of Stories involves lots of people working hard to make the project a success. Spread the Word would like to take this opportunity to thank a number of people involved.

Firstly, to the project funders Arts Council England, without the financial support City of Stories would not happen.

The Association of London Chief Librarians for their partnership and fellowship, particularly President Anthony Hopkins for his constant support and belief.

The fantastic participating library services and staff who were involved in the coordination and delivery of City of Stories:

Barking and Dagenham: Lena Smith and all at Barking Learning Centre

Bexley: Caroline Duckworth, Susan Prior and all at Bexleyheath Library

Brent: Sarah Smith and all at The Library at Willesden Green

Camden: Peter Baxter, Sam Eades and all at St Pancras Library

Croydon: David Herbert and Joan Redding and all at Croydon Central Library

Ealing: Shanthi Ahailathirunayagam, Martha Lambert and all at Ealing Library

Greenwich: Richard Davidson, Tatyana D'Souza, Tony Maryon and all at Woolwich Library

Hackney: Monica Sever, Calum Docherty and all at Stoke Newington Library

Hammersmith and Fulham: David Harland, Jodie Green and all at Hammersmith and Fulham Library

Islington: Tony Brown and all at Islington Central Library

Kensington and Chelsea: Leanne Bellott and all at Kensington Central Library

Kingston: Alison Townsend, Joanne Moulton and all at Kingston Central Library

Lewisham: Antonio Rizzo, Kat Blench, Simon Higgs, Stephen Bruce and all at Forest Hill Community Library

Merton: Maggie Nightingale, Anthony Hopkins and all at Merton Arts Space at Wimbledon Library

Newham: Deborah Peck and all at Canning Town Library

Redbridge: Nina Simon and all at Redbridge Central Library

Tower Hamlets: Richard Bolt, Kate Pitman and all at Idea Store Whitechapel

Waltham Forest: Muhammed Javed, Kadriye Cenk and all at Walthamstow Central Library

Westminster: Amy Houtenbos, Laurence Foe and all at Victoria Library

Wandsworth: Chris Dobb, Jeremy Travers and all at Balham and Putney Libraries

The City of Stories writers-in-residence, thank you for your incredible input, creativity and enthusiasm: Bidisha, Irenosen Okojie, Courttia Newland and Alex Wheatle.

The City of Stories writer-facilitators, thank you for your wise words, reliability and enthusiasm: Anita Belli, Miriam Nash, Jasmine Cooray, Lewis Buxton, Nick Field, Tom Mallender, Laila Sumpton and Erica Masserano.

Nick Ogden and all at High Six Media, thank you for making fantastic films.

Franek Wardynski, for your brilliant poster, flyer and book designs.

Aliya Gulamani at Spread the Word, for your fierce and astute coordination and energy.

And lastly, to everyone who attended City of Stories workshops, everyone who entered the competition and of course particular thanks to the winning and highly commended writers whose stories make this anthology a reality.